**The Good Dad** - I'm back home, taking care of my father in the hospital. I'm a good son, but I'm learning to be a good dad, too. Although I'm childless, I have Chase, a college boy who calls me 'Daddy.' He's a good kid, and when we get between the sheets, it's pure, raw passion.

**The Artist** - Edward, a Los Angeles cop-in-training, poses for an older artist who is impressed by his huge physique. Due to his size, Edward has never been with a girl, let alone a man. In the Academy locker room, Edward meets an older cop who proves that there's no such thing as too big.

**Tuxes n' Tails** - I'm Chris, and I just started working at the tuxedo shop downtown. Jon, my boss, is showing me the ropes. Then I catch him *in flagrante delicto* in the bathroom at work. Yeah, he's embarrassed, but he uses it as an excuse to teach me what it means to be a man, in every sense of the word.

**Joker's Wild** - Bo's got big problems. Young and penniless, disowned by his drunk father, he hops off the bus in Las Vegas, looking for a place to belong. He discovers that there's big money to be made for guys his size in Sin City. His high-rolling client, Noah, shows him how to gamble, how to enjoy sex, and what it feels like to have a loving daddy.

# COME YOUNG AND OLD

*Gay Age Gap Erotica*

J. W. STEED    PETER SCHUTES    CHUCK IDGAF

Come Young and Old
First Edition Printed 2025 by Peter Schutes Publishing.
The Good Dad Copyright © 2025 by J. W. Steed
The Artist Copyright © 2025 by Peter Schutes
Joker's Wild Copyright © 2025 by Peter Schutes
Tuxes n' Tails Copyright © 2025 by Chuck Idgaf
All Rights Reserved.

ISBN: 978-1-963667-23-3



The story, all names, characters, and incidents portrayed in this production are fictitious. No identification with actual persons (living or deceased), places, buildings, and products is intended or should be inferred.

Cover Illustration by Pipeman Doug

This book is for ADULT AUDIENCES ONLY. It contains substantial sexually explicit scenes with multiple partners and graphic language which may be considered offensive by some readers.

All sexual activity in this work is consensual and all sexually active characters are 18 years of age or older.

# CONTENTS

# THE GOOD DAD

## BY J. W. STEED

# A PORTRAIT OF CHASE

"Yes. Please. Just like that, Dad," whispers Chase. Dad, he likes to call me. A fictional conceit, as we first met only this week. Yet I don't mind the roleplay. I'm old enough to have sired him.

This college junior, all of twenty or twenty-one, skims along the twin-sized mattress with serpentine motion, back arched, lean hips raised. Scant fuzz below his navel grazes the rumpled sheets. In this artificial twilight born of blackout shades and drapes drawn tight, his skin is pale enough to give off its own faint luminescence, like foxfire on a summer's evening.

Yet again, I wrench apart the globes of his ass as I thrust inside. His hole is tight. So damned tight. It clutches at my shaft as back and forth I glide.

"Make it swell, Daddy." I clamp down on my pelvic floor and squeeze. The sudden alteration in girth makes him groan. His head lolls back; a shaggy fringe of dark, long hair tickles the top of his shoulders. Inside him, I thrust deep to enlarge myself once again. His chest collapses onto the bed, alarming the already creaking bedsprings. "Oh god." The light tenor of his voice is muffled by pillows and bedclothes. "I'm gonna shoot, Dad. Can I shoot? Please let me, Daddy."

I reach down and swat away his greedy hand from

his cock. Dad gets the privilege of saying when his boy can blast. From behind him, I spit in my hand and wrap it around the kid's meat. His shaved balls drape upon my wrist as I spread the slick fluid up and down the shaft. His howls of pleasure redouble in the tiny room's confines.

"I love you, Dad." Up I draw him until he rests upon my deep chest. Chase leans back, sinking into the downy mattress of my fur. At the sensation of my free hand caressing his smooth skin, he shivers and raises an arm high into the air. As every inch of him quakes and trembles at my touch, the boy's eyes open to look into mine. "I love you so much."

I nod, unblinking, connected by our locked stare. "I know you do."

His face softens, overcome with emotion. "Oh god. I love you. I love you, Dad." Soon he's buckling at my grip. A few twists of the wrist, a few vigorous strokes, and he begins spraying his load across the bedsheets. Anchored by my dick deep in his butt and my hand at the base of his spine, he buckles and thrashes as shot after shot of warm, sticky stuff cascades into my scooped fingers. The kid is loud. It's a good thing his family—his actual, biological family—isn't here in the home where he still lives to save money, or they'd be battering down the bedroom door.

At long last, he subsides. It seems a shame to wipe his semen onto the sheets, but more of a pity to let it go to waste. So, I pull out and slap the goo onto my engorged cock. The sound echoes with a wet smack. Then I shove it back in that open, sloppy hole. He knows what I want; his hips rise to meet me as I drill.

I fuck like I'm holding a grudge, like I want to punish instead of praise. I fuck like I don't care what bruises I create for either of us. It's not long before I, too, fill his little room with a roar.

Afterward, we take a moment to drowse in the half-dark as he cuddles close. Eventually, with a sigh, he nuzzles my armpit and glances at his watch. "I've got class in a half hour."

"It's okay, Son," I mumble. Three days Chase and I have met during our lunchtimes. I'm well aware of his midday schedule. The urban university he attends is a quick ten-minute drive.

"Mind if I shower?" He bounds up from the bed with sudden puppy vitality, making me feel every single minute of the—Christ—three decades that lie between us. All I have the energy to do is wave my hands to shoo him toward the little bathroom at one end of his untidy room.

A full-length mirror hangs inside the door; the kid doesn't seem to realize that from my angle on the bed, I can spy his every move beyond. I watch as he cups, then slaps his round little butt so that the flesh jiggles. I observe the mighty grin on his face when he probes his hole and discovers how wet his fingertips come away. I admire his slender body as he opens the shower stall and turns the tap.

While he waits for the hot water to arrive, he inspects his upper lip in the mirror over the sink. Upon the mirror, I watch as he grooms his micro-mustache. Baby's first facial hair. It's really no more than the most featherweight trimming of dark peach fuzz, perilously clinging to the ridge above his lip, barely visible beyond arm's length. I find endearing the care he takes in smoothing it down after the wrangling our mouths have enjoyed. Pleased with what he sees, he backs away from the mirror and bounces on the balls of his feet, arms outstretched, bobbing and swaying as—left-right, left-right, left-right-left—he punches at the air. For a silent minute he boxes with an invisible opponent, eyes on himself in the sink mirror, his little cock springing up and down. Finally, he grins in the glass, chucks himself softly on the chin, and disappears behind the shower door.

This is how I hope to remember Chase when eventually our paths part ways: lively and unselfconscious, happy with what he sees in himself.

In the bathroom, the sounds of water cease; there's a near-silence once the kid turns off the overhead fan. That's my cue to haul myself up to a sitting position and fumble for my clothing. I'm pulling on a sock when he tackles me, his skin still damp. A sopping towel shimmies from his narrow waist onto the jumble of athletic footwear at the bed's foot. "Don't go," he teases, butting his wet hair against my shoulder.

He's so cute, this kid. The kiss I plant atop his head is rewarded by his shy smile. "What are you going to do? Tie me down and keep me?"

"Maybe." He crosses his skinny legs and leans into me. "Seriously. Don't go."

"I have to. So do you." I wrap my arms around him. "You've got class in..." I check my watch. "Twenty minutes."

"I can be late."

"You cannot," I insist, returning to the sock that dangles from my foot. "I've got to get back to my father."

# THREE DAYS EARLIER

"The chow here is great! You want some?"

I've cranked my pop's bed to an upright position. He sits with his tray table pulled close to his chest as he shovels down lunch. For some reason, Pop enjoys hospital food. No, he fucking *loves* hospital food. He thinks it's top-notch, lip-smackin', gourmet grub. Pour some diluted canned chicken noodle in a cup, slap down succotash and a slice of institutional meatloaf with a watery gravy on a plate, top it off with a sealed plastic tub of vanilla pudding, and serve everything on a tray with plastic utensils, and the man is in hog heaven.

I decline his offer. We're in week two of his latest round of medical misadventures in as many hospitals. Two weeks, and I'm four hundred miles away from home, taking care of him as best he lets me.

The old man had called my cell Sunday before last saying he'd felt funny. He didn't sound like his usual self; it took me several minutes to coax him into admitting he had problems walking. He refused my advice to see a doctor. Living on his own for so long has turned him into a stubborn old mule. I immediately threw some clothes in a suitcase and drove seven hours to drag him to urgent care.

"What can a doc-in-a-box tell me that I don't know

already?" he'd snapped and snarled. Even in the exam room, he'd been uncooperative. When the doctor there had suggested I take Pop to an emergency room as soon as possible, I'd listened.

The twelve hours that followed were some of the most unpleasant of my life. In a cold exam room, we'd waited, Pop carping and complaining nonstop between tests while I'd stared at the diminishing battery icon on my phone. At two in the morning, a serious-looking physician finally gave us the news: my father had suffered not one, but two minor strokes and required immediate hospitalization followed by a stint after in the rehab hospital to get back his mobility.

In the space of the few seconds it took for the doctor to make his pronouncement, my short trip south was commuted into a sentence of indefinite duration. No one else can be here for him. Everything's up to me.

A rehab hospital is where he is now. It's a one-level sprawl shaded by old oaks that's older than other rehab options, but cheerful and easy to navigate. Pop's private room is bigger than my living room and kitchen combined, back in New York. The staff is uniformly upbeat, friendly, and professional. I commit to memory every single one of their names to use when thanking them. We spend the first afternoon engaging in an activity that my father will talk about with fond relish for months after: filling out a week's worth of meal requests.

For an hour and a half, I read out the menu choices for each upcoming meal while Pop considers big-picture questions like, what juice would he prefer with his breakfast on Thursday, tomato, orange, grapefruit, or apple? What should accompany his chicken cutlet, that night, macaroni and cheese? Or mashed potatoes? He smacks his lips over each culinary decision while nurses bring him applesauce.

He is living like a king.

It's the third day of his tenure that I snort a little,

sitting at his bedside. "What are you doing with your fancy phone?" Pop asks.

"Your hot nurse is on Grindr," I tell him. Said hot nurse is a mere 35 feet away.

"What's Grindr?"

We've discussed Grindr before, but my father's brain has little retention for anything not of direct interest to him. "It's a dating app for gay men. You fire it up and see who's nearby."

He peers at me. "Which hot nurse? Laura? Or the one who bosses me around?"

"Molly," I remind him. "Why would Laura and Molly be on an app for gay men? No, it's Lance, the blue-eyed one who runs the gym."

"He's hot?" Pop seems baffled at the idea.

"Have you seen his shoulders?" I whistle with admiration.

"You and I have very different definitions of hot," he grumbles.

"Time for your physical therapy, hon." Molly, the nurse who shows up to take the invalid to his appointments, strides into the room pushing a wheelchair. "Who's hot, now?"

"Lance." Pop and I speak simultaneously.

"That's for certain." With an economy of motion, Molly locks the chair into place, whisks aside the tray table, and sets the bed's whirring. She nods her rust-colored curls in affirmation. "Let's sit you up, then we'll get you into the chair."

A message pops up. It is not, sadly, from Lance. *Looking?*

Blank profiles are an exercise in diminishing returns. I won't interact with them. Mr. Looking, however, immediately follows up a photo, taken in the full-length mirror on a bathroom door. He's a young guy of twenty or twenty-one, slender, his chicken legs speckled with dense, wiry fur, his chest smooth, his face nearly covered by a mop of chin-length, dark, wavy hair. Even though he's nude in the shot, and even though he's turned sideways to show off the surprising roundness of his butt and the silhouette of his hanging dick, there's something in the defiant intent of his expression that makes him seem, well, shy.

Yet he'd come out from behind the anonymity of a blank profile to shoot his shot my way. I find it both flattering and irresistible. He's only five hundred feet away. Probably lives in the residential neighborhood behind the hospital parking lot.

*I'm free either lunchtimes or after 6*, I tell the kid, as Molly maneuvers my father into the wheelchair. He's scheduled daily for a ninety-minute-long appointment in the gym at twelve-thirty, followed by another hour after of occupational therapy. I've been using that block of time to get out and get some food and unwind from the institutional environment.

*Lunchtimes are great!* he replies. *My folks are home after 5:30 nights, but at work now. Come over if you want.*

Near the doorway, Pop is fussing about wearing the wrong sweater. Molly shuts down his protests with a word and pushes his chair into the hallway. *I definitely want. I'm free now. Send me an address.*

When I shove my phone into the pocket of my jeans, I'm surprised to find Molly standing over me. "I thought I'd give you a heads up." Her tone of institutional drollery presages bad news. "The staff here are concerned that your father may not be participating in his own recovery to the extent we wish."

He's being lazy, in other words. "He's a hard-headed old bastard," I translate, keeping my voice low so he won't overhear. "Who doesn't want to do the work?"

Her curt nod tells me I've hit the mark. "Look. His insurance is good, and we're not threatening to kick him out. But his long-term outcome won't be great if he doesn't invest in his own—I think you know what I'm saying."

"Thank you, Molly." Absolutely, I understand. My

father needs to treat his tenure here less as a spa stay and more as an opportunity to put in the work. "I've been telling him already, but I'll keep at it. He's just—"

Her acknowledgment is sympathetic. We exchange a wry smile as she rejoins Pop in the hallway.

In my pocket, the phone vibrates. I've got a lunchtime appointment to keep.

❧ 3 ❧

# FIRST MEETING

Two blocks from the rehab hospital, in the suburban ranch house where he lives, the boy named Chase and I sit side by side upon his twin bed. His dark and quiet personal space is a contrast to the bright tidiness of the rooms I had to pass through to get here. His family living room has the blandly stylish appearance of an Ashley Furniture showcase. The kid's bedroom, though, is plainly the space of someone who's never had to look after himself.

It's not squalid. It doesn't stink. Shoes lie in an unsorted pile at the foot of his bed, though, kicked off and left where they tumble. The closet hangs open; it's difficult to tell where the hamper of dirty clothing ends and the potentially clean garments begin. The walls are painted a deep blue and covered with posters, half from anime with which I'm unfamiliar, half with promotional posters for old Final Fantasy video games. I'm definitely within the quarters of a post-adolescent boy.

He's nervous, now I'm here. Trembling, even. I'm aware I should be making the first move. Young men who reach out to me expect a certain level of sexual mastery—they desire a masculine dad type as a guide. Someone who knows what to do and say, every step of the way. Normally, that's a role I happily play. With this skinny kid that I've just met, though, I'm less certain.

He's an attractive boy. I mean, that mop of messy hair is something that gets me every time, both in the gut and groin. Those pretty eyes, those big, wide eyes, those serious eyes. Sidelong, they stare my way.

Shit. He's pretty.

From his photos, I have an idea what lies beneath that oversized tee, below those baggy skater shorts. If he were an actor, he'd be cast in a romcom as the sensitive and artistic best friend of some female college freshman, no doubt played by a former Disney star. Or —and it unsettles me as I consider it—have Wardrobe throw a hoodie over his head and smudge circles beneath his eyes, as the tortured loner prodded into a school shooting.

No, don't think about that. Fuckin' Gen Z'ers. So difficult, with their puritanical views. I've never seen anyone as afraid of sex as these young whippersnappers. I'd lay a hand on him now, but he's vibrating like a fawn that's spotted a hunter, eyes wide, unsure which way to bolt.

Fuck. Maybe this was a mistake.

His long, naked toes wriggle against the loop pile of his bedroom rug. I clear my throat and place a hand in the middle of the kid's back. "Look," is all I say, prepared to apologize and make a polite departure.

Then he lunges. His fingers encircle my skull; with hunger, he pulls my face to his and engulfs me in a kiss. His mouth tastes sweet, like bubble gum. Once he's wrenched me atop him, once he feels my weight pressing down upon his slender frame, he sighs happily as we kiss. His hands dive beneath my tee while his legs curl around my hips, locking me close.

All right then. Way to go, Gen Z.

We wrestle to find comfortable positions on the narrow mattress. Piece by piece, our clothing arcs through the air and lands upon the mountain of sneakers on the floor. My beard abrades his skin, drawing satisfying gasps. His lips search for far-flung parts of my body while I poke and prod his soft flesh. "Please," he breathes, when I clutch and squeeze one of his pert little buttocks. That breathing turns to rasps when I sit him squarely on my face, where he rakes and squirms as my tongue savages his pucker. Soon he's leaning forward to suck me, expertly taking my shaft to the root.

I need to unload. I shove the kid off and yank up his hips. I'm about to plunge inside him for the first time when he puts a hand on my chest to stop me. His knuckles tug at my fur. For a moment, we remain still, captured in what must look like some advanced couples yoga pose with a name like The Wheelbarrow or The Farmer and His Plow. He looks up the slant of his body into my eyes. "Can I ask for something weird?"

There's weird, then there's what inexperienced kids like Chase think is weird. "What?"

"Can I say I love you, when you fuck me?" My lips part, surprised. I'd thought he wanted me to spit in his mouth or something. "You don't have to say it back," he adds in haste, terrified he's gone too far. "I'm not gonna be a freak about it or anything. I won't stalk you. I just...I just..."

My voice is level as I finish his sentence. "You need to be able to say those words to someone."

He nods, almost ashamed I can read his mind. "Is it okay?" For answer, I keep my eyes upon his while I spit once more into my hand and rub it onto his already-slick hole. Then, slowly, gently, sweetly, I slide myself inside, inch by inch. The kid's lips part. His eyes become lidded once more. "I love you, Dad," he says in a tentative whisper when I reach bottom.

"I didn't hear you, Son."

He understands the permission I'm giving him. "I love you, sir."

I nod, acknowledging his words. I'll tolerate them. They're just another form of role play.

And the boy is heartbreakingly cute.

When was the last time I fucked? Vaguely, I re-member meeting a guy in a rugby shirt at the 9th Av-enue Saloon after our hands met over a bowl of burnt popcorn. He had a beefy butt that I filled while he begged me to keep the noise down so his roommate wouldn't hear. His bathroom had been so dirty and cov-ered with grime that I'd deliberately lost the number he'd given me.

So, three weeks? Longer than usual. I should be pounding away like crazy, but some instinct makes me hold back. I'm loving the feel of this kid's tight hole. The velvet clutch of him. So damned tight, seizing at my meat like he was made for it. The contrast between us turns me on: my dense chest hair grinding and scraping against his pale, skinny back. The sight of my angry pole sodomizing his pink pucker. His flute-like gasps. My guttural growls. Everything about this scene should be making me slam him midway into next November.

Yet, I hold back. For the moment, I'm content to grind, bush to hole, as I observe his responses. His eyes closed, he arches his back, opening himself to take me. His nostrils flare as he exhales deeply, releasing what-ever tensions have built up, anticipating this meeting. Gooseflesh prickles his skin; his face reddens as I pepper his shoulders with soft kisses. I might be three weeks dry, but he seems to have been without for much longer.

I withdraw, ignoring his protests. "I'm going to lay back on your bed, Son," I tell him, pulling myself into a seated position, a pillow cushioning my upper spine against the headboard. "And I want you to ride."

He nods, eager to resume the connection. I'm sur-prised when he impales himself with vigor on my cock, but he seems to crave the shock and ache of being split open. My hands rest first upon his furry little legs, then cup the back of my head as I allow him to buck and rub his ass lips against the root of my meat. "You like that, don't you?" I ask. When he nods, I emphasize, "You like it. Don't you, Son?"

His eyes flash open. "Yes, Dad. I love it. I love your cock." His own pecker, pert and cute and fun-sized, bobs and sways as he bounces. There's trouble in his eyes, though. I can tell he's working his way back around to the words he needs to say. I nod, giving him permission. "I love the way you feel inside."

"And?"

I don't need to pound when he's doing all the work for me. "And I love knowing your sperm is going to fill me up."

"And..." I'm breathless, myself. He's bringing me perilously close, with that wild buckling.

"I love how hot and sexy you are, Dad." Once again, he indulges in running his hands through my fur, over my beard, riffling the bristles of my short hair. "Do I make you feel good?"

"Oh, baby boy," I breathe, feeling myself lose more and more control with every new clutch of his hole. "You have no idea how good you feel."

"You're my dad," he whispers. His hips grow more insistent. He's determined to get this load out of me, and he's going to win. Seeing me helpless beneath him makes him grow more confident. "I love you. I love you so much."

"Say it," I demand.

"I love you, Dad." Liquid fire blasts from my nuts to slick the walls of his chute. Still, Chase grinds, reveling in the sensation of my load as it lubes him. "Oh, fuck. There it is. My dad's seed. My dad's seed, filling me up. I love you. I love you."

For a few moments I cannot see; all the blood rushing to my dick makes my vision swim. I'm aware, though, of hot liquid spurting onto my collarbone, my shoulders, my chest. When finally the tide recedes and my vision is once more sharp, I meet the boy's eyes and regard him with astonishment. I don't think I've ever shot so hard in my life.

"Did you like it, Dad?" Uncertainty makes his voice waver a little.

"Oh, baby boy," I tell him, as I nod. "Did you?"

His sigh tells me everything I know. "Come back tomorrow?" he asks, as gravity sinks him into my waiting embrace.

I'm a little surprised at how quickly and completely he relaxes against my chest; he blankets me with trust and warmth. "I will," I promise.

# 4

# THE COMFORTS OF HOME

"God damn it." In the hallway outside his door, Pop clutches onto the grab bar for dear life. "Doesn't anybody do any goddamn work in this goddamn place? Hello? *Hello!* I want the hell out of here!"

"Where are you going to go?" I'm standing nearby and not making any effort to help. He's upright, at least. A week of physical therapy has done that much for him.

Growing up, I'd always been grateful Pop was the most even-keeled of men. The only time I'd seen the man lose his temper had been maybe when the Orioles were on a losing streak. This last week in rehab, though, had brought out the infant in him. This is merely the latest of his many tantrums. At least it's timed well, with no one around to witness: the staff are well down the hallway in the break room, celebrating Molly's birthday.

"Home!" he snaps.

"How are you going to get there? I'm not taking you. You can't drive. Are you planning to catch a bus? Walk?" He scowls at me. In pointing out the obvious, I've become the enemy. "Who's going to take care of you once you're back? Not me. You check yourself out early, and you'll be on your own. I'll go. Look." My tone modulates as I attempt to bargain with the obstinate old mule. "All the work you've done this week has gotten you back on your feet enough to throw this stupid conniption. That's progress. They're saying in another week, you might be able to get around with only a cane. How about I get your walker, you get back to your bed, and we stop this nonsense?"

"I'm getting out." With his shoulders, he dodges my attempts to get a hold on him. "You're not stopping me."

"Come on, now." In my mind, I'm replaying all my childish furies, back in my old school days. None of them were as bad as this outburst of temper.

For a brief moment, he stumbles; I spring forward, convinced his legs are going to give out. But he still has a firm grip on the grab bar. When I get too close, he warns me off with a final salvo. "You're denying me the comforts of home," the old man spits, as with sheer force of will, he remains upright.

I have been so lonely these last two weeks. I'm an empty well, echoing, dry, with its walls on the verge of collapse. All my energy I've poured into hospital visits and doctor consultations and making certain Pop has what he needs. Evenings, I work on installing the hardware that Leticia the occupational therapist suggests, to get his home ready for his eventual return.

Throughout this ordeal, from home to hospital to rehab, not once has my father acknowledged all I'm doing. He takes my back-breaking efforts for granted. That alone is fine—he can, and should, assume I'll be there when he needs. But fuck, would it ever be nice to hear a thank you from his lips. Thank you for helping me through this mess. Thank you for taking notes. Thank you for remembering and explaining my complex medical history to every new caregiver we encounter.

A boy I've known less than a week tells me every afternoon he loves me. The dad I've known for fifty years, for whom I've put my life on hold? Not once during this whole crisis.

But would I do it again, make that drive, wreck my neck and back on a hotel mattress, knowing how cantankerous and outright mean he'd be? Yeah. You bet your ass I would. Things might have changed between us, but he's my dad, and he needs me.

That's why I take a deep breath. Close my eyes. Summon some patience. Then, in the gentlest possible manner, I say, "Relax. Let me help."

Fire ignites his eyes, but just for a moment. He unbends enough to allow me to pry him from the grab bar. As he leans into me, arms around my neck, together we stumble back down the hall to his room. A few minutes later, back in his bed, he's still grumbling, but he's gracious enough to wish Molly a happy birthday when the staff returns from their quick break.

*I can't get out to see you today,* I text Chase with genuine regret. *My pop is acting up, and I should stick around.* I am a bottomless pit of loneliness. An attractive boy's affection is an anodyne I welcome.

An ellipsis almost instantly appears as the boy pecks out a response. Then, after a moment, it vanishes. I've disappointed him, too, I imagine. But a moment later, it appears again, followed by a message. *Let me come to your hotel tonight, then?* A moment after that, *Please Dad?*

*Yeah*, I say, surprised at how quickly my heart starts beating. *I'll be free after nine.* I shove my phone back into my jeans pocket, feeling a little better about the day.

I am in need of kindness, no matter how cosmetic.

# 5

## TIES THAT BIND

P *arking in the lot outside now, sir.*

I'm lying on the king-sized bed in my hotel room, naked in the dark, when the text lights up my phone on the table next to me. Its light illuminates the popcorn ceiling above. My cock comes to life, slowly lolling to one side and growing heavier and thicker. I've already considered how I'm going to reply, so with speed, I thumb out a response.

*Dad's taking a nap in 208, Son. Let yourself in.*

After I hit send, I spring to my feet and pad across the carpet. My cock bounces and swings with every step. I angle my body so that it's mostly hidden from the hall when I pull open the door, then I swing the security latch so that it prevents the door from shutting all the way. Prepared, I scamper back to the bed, dive under the comforter, and arrange myself into a slumbering position: flat on my back, hands raised above my head, head tilted to one side.

While I wait, I take stock. I've set lube on the bedside table, next to a couple of hand towels. Despite the bright street sign of the gym next door, with the blackout curtain drawn, the room exists in perpetual twilight. My cock ring presses snug against my balls. This position is stupid, though. Who sleeps on his back with his arms over his head like some cheesy vintage porn? Onto my side I flop, as I tuck one of the many hotel pillows under the crook of my neck and pull the comforter up to my chin. This is how I really sleep.

My room isn't far from the elevator. Through the sliver of open door, I hear the grind of mechanics. A ding. A pad of footsteps as they approach. For a moment, the room brightens as the door opens; then darkens again as my visitor softly shuts it and flips the latch. I consider closing my eyes to feign sleep—but why deny myself the sight of his shadowed figure kicking off his sneakers, removing footie socks? I watch as Chase drops a baseball cap onto the floor and crosses his arms to seize the hem of his t-shirt. There's a crackle of static as he pulls it off, then lets it drop where he stands.

The shorts and briefs he discards last. He steps out of both in one fluid motion, his back to me. I've been fucking and eating that ass all week, but seeing it pale, round, and blue in the room's gloom takes my breath away. My dick pulses, fully hard.

I close my eyes and simulate slumber when he turns. I feel a rush of cool air as the bedclothes lift. Quietly, softly, as if he's genuinely fearful of waking me, the boy crawls into my bed and slides close. I feel a hand groping my midsection. It connects with my hip, slides to my rigid dick. Then a mouth, warm and wet, wraps around my cock. I allow the boy to suck me for a moment or two before I stir. "Who's there?" I ask sleepily.

He releases his hold on my meat and slides up until his head rests on my pillow. "It's me, Dad. Chase. Your son."

"Chase?" I ask. "What're you doing in my bed?"

"I had a bad dream and couldn't sleep." There's an earnest and even innocent yearning in his whispering that moves me. It moves my cock, too, so that it butts against his hard stomach. "I didn't mean to wake you up."

"A bad dream? That's no good, kiddo." My fingers riffle his lank hair. "What did you dream about?"

"I dreamed you told me I couldn't suck your dick anymore, Dad." As if addressed personally, my meat springs up to demand its due. I feel his fingers wrap around its girth as he nestles against my furry chest. "It made me real sad."

My reply is gruffer than I expect, but desire makes me hoarse. "Aw, Son. That will never happen."

"You promise? Really, Dad—do you promise?"

In the space of a moment, the mood has shifted. I'd thought we were engaging in some lighthearted role-playing. Absolute sincerity now colors his questions, though. I know it would be heartless to run roughshod over any hopes he might have. Yet I will have to return home north, someday. I choose my words with care. "There might be times you and I won't be able to see each other," I admit, as he grips me tightly. "But that doesn't change the fact that I'm your dad. Dad will always take care of you when he's able."

In response, he presses his mouth against mine. His sinewy arms snake around my chest, drawing me close. When I slide my tongue through his open lips, he trembles with excitement. My hands roam up and down his body. Smooth flesh grazes my palms when I slide them across his ribs; further down, his butt and legs give way to wiry fur. His eyes remain closed as we make out; he sighs and shivers as my hands discover new places to explore.

A switch flips. I've had enough of this sweetness, this role-playing. I am going to take this kid, shove his face into the pillow, mount his furry ass, and get myself buried deep. No more monkeying around. Wrestling off the bedclothes takes a moment, but at last I expose both our bodies to the hotel room's chill and lay my hands upon Chase's shoulders, prepared to toss him onto his stomach. I growl, "Time to take it like a good boy."

Instead, I find myself flat on my back, gasping for air. Somehow, the little punk has done the flipping; he straddles my hips and presses his hands into my chest. At first, I can't even hear what he's saying because my ears are surrounded by pillow. "What?" I ask, confused.

"I said, nah."

"Nah?" I don't get it. "You came to get that little ass fucked."

"I came," he says with the patience of a teacher speaking to an exceptionally uncooperative child, "to be with my dad. Now." I have no choice but to exhale when he presses his full weight on my chest. "Do you trust me?"

"Trust you?"

"Yes or no question, mister." He leans way back to grab something from the bed's bottom, I suppose tossed there when I'd been pretending to sleep. When he returns to his upright posture, from one hand dangles a pair of closed loops connected by a metal chain. Handcuffs. Fabric and Velcro, the kind you buy at a cheap mall novelty store. From the other hangs a length of dark fabric. At first, I think it's a sleep mask, but then light dawns. He's brandishing a blindfold. "Do you trust me?"

I can't help myself. Visions of all the bad things that could happen flicker through my mind. My phone's still on the bedside table, my wallet in the jeans folded atop the desk, my laptop in my backpack, sitting on the chair. True, if the kid made away with any of my stuff, I know where he lives—but that's assuming I'm alive enough to track him down. I don't know what Chase intends, exactly, but even in a pair of Velcro cuffs, it's fraught with risk.

Yet my cock stands erect, inflamed both from the heat of his backside and the smolder of his gaze, visible even in this darkness. I truly want to let him do whatever it is he has in mind.

He must sense my hesitation, because he leans

down to kiss me. Those soft lips against mine are the best argument he could make. "Relax, Dad," he whispers. "Let me take care of you."

Surely, it's coincidence. I'd used similar words myself that afternoon. If I needed a sign, though, this is as good as it's going to get. Looking him square in the eyes, I moisten my suddenly dry lips and speak through a cracked voice. "Yes." I nod with emphasis. "I trust you."

"That's a good dad." There's amusement in his voice as he leans over to grab my arm. One of the cuffs fastens snugly around my wrist; he pats down the fasteners with a crunch. "Hmm."

He muses a moment as he inspects the environment as best as he can, dark as it is. My arm wrenches upward. Though the bed has its padded headboard affixed to the wall—it's a classy joint with a waffle maker in the complimentary breakfast buffet, after all—there's a metal support bar at its base running across its width, with just enough space for him to hook the other soft loop and the chain attaching it. I willingly offer my free wrist for confinement and am rewarded with a smile as he smooths tight the tiny hooks into their soft, receptive loops.

And that's it. He's got me restrained, hands over my head. I give my fetters an experimental tug and hear the chain rattle against the metal bar. I won't be going anywhere. "Looks like you got me where you want me, Son." My voice grates. I'm hoarse. My heart pounds like a steam hammer. My erection is already cement hard and yearns for release. This state of arousal is actually painful. I'm shocked by how excited I am at such a small loss of control. What's going to happen when he covers my eyes?

I'm about to find out.

"Ssshh," Chase whispers comforts into my ear as the padded cups press on either side of my nose. I wasn't aware I'd been mouthing soft protests until I heard him quieting me. "It's all for you," he chides. "Everything I do is for you, Dad."

His wrists brush against my temples; I feel straps surround my head and dig against the tops of my ears. Another crunch of Velcro as he smooths down the fasteners. It was dark before, but crap. This is blackness at an entirely different level. Crazy, how a simple strip of cloth and foam can unmoor me from reality: I feel set adrift, almost floating without gravity, all sense of direction lost. Even up and down no longer have meaning. When in my alarm I thrash slightly, I remember my wrists are anchored above my head. The chain rasps along the bar.

Am I panicking? Oh, lord. I'm panicking. Heat prickles at my armpits, my thighs, the very soles of my feet. I know how outsized my reaction is, but I can't help myself. I'm not completely cut off from the world. I can hear Chase's gentle assurances, feel his soft kisses on cheeks and forehead, smell his familiar scent of soap and body spray. I can still sense the boy's weight atop me, his hand upon my chest, another hand reaching back to wrap itself around my length. My cock isn't suffering, either—it still rages, still has its own agenda, unaware of anything going on a few feet north of its location.

"You all right?" he says, checking in.

No, I'm not all right. I hate this helplessness. I am a man used to being in control, to setting the pace. All I want to do is order the boy to remove the cuffs, to strip off the layer of fabric occluding my sight. I'm so close to anger, too. Hampered even slightly, I risk turning surly. Maintaining my temper is taking all my energy.

It doesn't take much to render a man completely helpless, does it? A pair of soft cuffs. A blindfold. Tinier still yet infinitely more significant, a clot of blood in the brain stem, smaller than a pinpoint.

But I am far more fortunate than my father, I realize in this moment. What hampers me is voluntary; I can banish it with a single request. The best thing I can do is to vanquish this silly state of panic and accept my boy's offer of pleasure. Let Chase have what he wants. I am a lucky man, able to afford enduring a little uncertainty.

I consider my response before licking my lips. "I guess I'm all yours, kiddo."

I'm rewarded by the scent of his breath, still sweet from the gum he'd consumed between the parking lot and my room. Then by the soft, ticklish pressure of his lips against mine. I want to cup his head and stroke his hair, to draw him more deeply into my arms, but how quickly I've forgotten. My wrists chafe as the chain rattles once more against the metal crossbar. God damn it.

For now, I have to take consolation in what senses remain. His weight shifts off my midsection as Chase repositions himself to my left. I feel the tickle of his fingertips on my pecs, riffling through the thick carpet of fur there. He's always been fascinated by my chest hair. "You don't know how many times I used to fantasize about getting you naked and to myself, Dad." I gasp slightly as he applies pressure to my nipples with a pinch; my cock responds by leaping and straining into thin air. "I used to stare at your muscles and hope I grew up like you."

"You grew up real pretty, Son," I manage to say, distracted as I am by the trail of his soft lips down my abdomen. "No worries there."

"But I wanted to be more like you. A man." I feel the side of his face rest on my stomach. One of his hands rests on my thigh, the fingers nestled beneath my balls. My cock jumps at his proximity. Surely, he has to see how badly it needs attention. "A real man, I mean. You were perfection to me. Still are." Without warning, I feel first the brush of his long hair, then the heat of his breath, then the slick, wet sweetness of his tongue, in the juncture where leg meets pelvis.

"Oh damn, Son," I manage to sputter. Then, I gasp, unable to verbalize a reply.

He's using his mouth and tongue to make wet the crease at the top of my thigh. With two fingertips, he licks up my sac so that he can outline the border between taint and balls. He's deliberately teasing me on the margins of my erogenous zones, zeroing in on his destination with slow calculation. "You probably never knew how bad I wanted you." His quiet murmurs hypnotize me. Their quiet insistence rouses some hidden current of electricity that begins to buzz at the top of my scalp, sending impulses down my spine. "How I used to stare at you. How I used to watch you, when you'd take a nap." He kisses the seam running down the sac's center, making me gasp. "You don't think that's creepy, do you, Dad?"

I have to swallow, hard. "No, kiddo. That's not creepy at all."

"Good. Because I used to do it a lot." When he flicks out at one ball and gives it a loving swipe of his broad, wet tongue, I let out a cry. Breath from his satisfied chuckles raises a warm bloom on my damp skin. "I used to jack off in my room at night, fantasizing about you. And now look where I am." Another lick—another choked cry. "Right where I've always wanted to be."

"Please." I'll be begging soon, I know. I can't stand this tease.

He continues on with his role-playing fantasy, ignoring me. "Right here between my dad's strong, hairy legs. Looking at his big, manly..." Finally, I feel the satisfaction of one soft hand taking hold of my meat, right around the base. "His *enormous*...monster...cock."

My throat is suddenly parched. "Please," I repeat. "Son, I need..."

What I need isn't his priority, though. "Did you ever look at me, Dad?" When he releases me, I groan with thwarted desire. I feel him spread my legs and position himself between them. "Didn't you know how much I wanted you? Were you holding out on me?"

My frantic brain searches for the correct answer or at least, in this game of fantasy, the answer he wants most to hear. "You were always a beautiful boy—ah!" Whatever answer I improvise is cut short by the sensation of heat and wetness. Judging from the tickle of his hair on my hips, he's opened wide and engulfed me with his mouth.

"You should've fucked me." Now his hand travels up and down my length, his fist wrapped tight. Again, I feel the furnace of his mouth as it slides back and forth, then coolness as he surfaces for air. "You should have come to my room at night and fucked me, Dad."

"I—I didn't know..." My protest is meek.

He's soaked me thoroughly by now. Spit is running down my shaft, tickling a scrotum that rises and falls at its own whim. "A good dad would have known." Another assault by his mouth that leaves me writhing in helpless pleasure, wrists straining against their confinement. "A good dad takes care of business."

"I try to be good," I protest. It's true. I do try to be good. To my partners. To Chase. To my dad. Doing the right thing is my go-to.

"I'm gonna have to take things in my own hands, I guess." Gone is that shy Gen X-er who could barely talk to me as we sat side by side, the afternoon I first met him. I've created some kind of sexual aggressor, a boy who takes what he wants.

I can't deny I like it. "You've gotta do what you've gotta do, Son." Every time I mention our putative relationship, his libido surges. Even blind, I can tell how overcome he is with desire. I feel his fingers grapple to find my cock . . . which isn't much of a feat, as it's been ramrod erect and searching for something warm the entire time he's been straddled over me. "The sooner, the—"

He cuts short the conclusion of my apothegm by

shoving several fingers in my mouth. Three, I quickly learn, from my tongue running over them. "Gotta get your boy ready," he says, now leaning down to growl in my ear. His free hand curls around my skull to cup my head, forcing my mouth wider as he shoves in more deeply. "Make those fingers wet. Need to get myself open and lubed for my dad's big dick. That's right." He seems to relish the gargling noises he's eliciting. "Nice... and...wet." Once he's withdrawn, I waggle my jaw and cough, trying to recover from the invasion. His weight shifts forward, onto my chest. He must be reaching around to his backside. "Fuck," he whispers. "My dad's spit, making me wet."

"Son..."

"I need you inside me, sir." Once again, he adjusts his position, freeing himself from my body. Ordinarily, my M.O. is to take a lot longer to get to this point. I love to fuck, but with a boy like this, I provide an experience to remember. I relish the dirty talk, the kissing, the promises of what I intend to deliver. I enjoy getting Chase excited, letting my own precum flow and lube my shaft as I flip the boy over then gnaw at his pucker until he groans and begs for me to open him up.

This hungry faggot has his own agenda, though. He guides me to the vicinity of his hole, lifts his hips. I know what's coming next.

Or at least, I think I do. I'm anticipating the meeting of tip to hole, followed by the gradual accommodation of a tight chute as my thick hardness stretches its walls. What I get is the last thing I expect. Chase aligns my shaft to his point of entry, then simply impales himself in one violent motion. There's no gradual anything, in his haste to engulf my entire eight-plus inches. One second my cock is exposed to the heater's gentle breeze; the next it's roughly swallowed by this boy's hole.

Chase lets out a mighty groan as he slams down on me; it's not entirely from pleasure. He could've done himself some damage, had I not been so rigid or aligned so perfectly. But my dick's still intact, and after a moment, he begins rocking back and forth, gathering speed and momentum as he recuperates.

"Fuck," I whisper. In response, he plants his hands upon my chest for counterbalance. "You really needed that."

"I needed to feel my daddy's cock rip me wide open." A hand runs over my beard. "Do I feel good enough, sir?"

"Oh, Son." Instinctively, I try to reach to cup his chin and cheek. Once again, the restraints nearly yank my arm from its socket. "You have always been more than good enough."

I might not be able to reach for him, but my interlocked fingers can support the back of my head when once more he leans down to kiss me. My tongue bores deep into his mouth; his hands cup the sides of his face. "So good," he whispers. Then he leans backward, my thighs detecting where he plants his hands onto the mattress.

He begins bucking wildly. The boy has great ass control. I can tell he's trying to do some fancy milking of my dick, but it's the sheer tightness that renders me even more helpless than the restraints around my wrists. Though his flesh inside is as warm and sweet as a summer peach plucked from a sun-drenched branch, the hole itself is rubber-band tight. Every thrust seems to rasp down the entire length of my shaft; nerves carry pleasure to every millimeter as his chute clamps and loosens and his hips gyrate to and fro. I know I'm pumping out precum, because his ass grows more and more slippery as insistently, he grinds.

There are limits to how high I can lift myself, but I strain upward, mouth open. "Please," I beg, hoping to be kissed. Instead, Chase propels himself up and shoves one of his nipples between my lips. Immediately, I apply suction, teasing it with my tongue. He likes them lightly chewed, I've learned, so I apply my incisors to the hairless little nubs, squeezing just the right amount. His ass becomes a vise. Fingers claw at the back of my skull. I gnaw a little harder. His body spasms; his lungs expel a low groan. All I have to do in order to tighten that already-taut hole is graze harder. I can turn his volume from zero to ninety with the tiniest of nibbles.

"This is everything," he breathes at last. "Thank you for letting me tie you up, Dad."

"Let me go?" I beg. There's so much more I could do, unrestrained.

He doesn't deny me outright, but neither does he grant my request. "So, you never, ever looked at me, Dad?"

"How could I not look at you? I'm the father of the most beautiful boy in the world," I say, giving the nipples another kiss, another light bite.

He clenches, moans, and begins to pick up the pace. "Did you really used to think that?"

"I still do."

I hope he can read the truth in my words—even if it's our own truth we create, as we go along.

"This will be our little secret?"

"Oh yes. Definitely our secret." I whimper as he clamps down.

"Nobody needs to know my daddy shoves his massive cock up my anus, right?"

I shake my head with vigor. "No, you definitely shouldn't mention that your dad loves stretching your beautiful little butthole."

"Good boys keep secrets."

"You'll always keep ours, Son."

Spinning this fantasy, detail by detail, excites him. The wetness on my abdomen surely has to be spooling from the tip of his cock. As up and down he gyrates on my dick, the pool of sticky stuff he's leaking barely has time to cool before he adds another glob. "I just need my dad to keep pumping his seed in me forever."

"Greedy." When I say the word, he clenches down on my meat, as if attempting to wrench it from my body to forever keep as his own.

"Greedy for you," he whispers. "Dad."

"Yeah?" By now, I've resigned myself to my limited range of motion. Instead, I'm relishing the other details left me: the rolling waves of the mattress, the sweet scent of cock in hole, the purr of the room's HVAC unit scoring our back-and-forth banter. "You don't say those pretty words to other daddies?"

"Only," he reiterates, then pauses as he draws his ass up to just below the crown of my dick before slamming back down as roughly as he had upon first taking me. "For you, sir."

"How about those sweet kisses, Son?"

"Those," Chase breathes, as he leans down and plants one on my lips, "are only for you."

Our mouths devour each other. It may be a fantasy we're weaving, but we're spinning it together, in the moment. We're constructing something demonstrably false: a tissue of lies based upon nothing but desire and longing. Yet right then, with every word, with every thrust, with every kiss and fumble and groan, we create something greater than the mere two of us. Our own truth. Our own reality, contained entirely in the dark of that hotel room. Our mutual fantasy: perfumed with sweat and testosterone, written in the salty prickle of precum, sealed by his lips against mine.

He is a greedy boy. Up and down his hole slams on my cock. He knows what he wants. He's determined to get it. When it arrives, my semen jets into him, erupting almost painfully, thick and molten. From side to side, I jerk and convulse, straining at the cuffs. The chain connecting them scrapes the metal bar with a screech. "I can feel it, Dad," he grunts, as I buck and struggle beneath him. He holds me down, keeps me from moving, as he shifts his determined grinding to a shorter, swifter rhythm. "I can feel you shooting. My dad's seed, deep in my guts. Fuck."

I gargle out words, but they make no sense. I'm lost in my orgasm. Shuddering. Shaking. Wrestling to catch my breath. My boy's cock flops up and down to strike my belly like a mallet attacks the tight skin of a timpani. And then, on one of its pendulous thuds as my own waves of pleasure subside, it erupts. His seed jets out, splatting onto my face, marking the pillows, covering my chest, then finally, slowly, oozing out onto my belly. I can't see it, but I can feel every jet when the spray hits me like a fire hose.

We're both breathing heavily. Trying to reorient ourselves. Moistening our lips, wiping the sweat from our eyes. Is this going to be the moment when the fantasy dissipates, and our exchanges become polite small talk? Or will we continue creating our own world together?

"Dad," he says. My dick still nestles within him—diminished slightly, but not soft. Though he's too spent to continue bucking and thrashing, his hips gyrate gently, tracing an infinity sign along the horizontal plane above my pelvis. "Did I do a bad thing? Tying you up, I mean?"

I give the question the consideration it deserves. How quick I'd been to anger at the first irritations of confinement. I'd needed to lash out. To punish. I hated being diminished.

My hesitation makes him worry. His hips move a little more slowly. "I just wanted to do something for you. Just for you. And the other day we joked about restraints. If it wasn't something you wanted..."

My tongue has to moisten my lips to get them to work. "No," I say, thrusting upward to spark his grinding into motion once more. "You did right, Son. You gave me exactly what I needed."

His weight shifts; I feel fumbling at my wrists, the sound of ripping Velcro. Then freedom. Together, we slide the blindfold from my eyes. I'm old enough to be afflicted with a little stiffness in the arms when I allow them to flop by my side, but it's only a moment before I pull myself up on my elbows to meet him face to face. "I love you, Dad," he whispers.

It's the first time he's said the words this evening, I realize. Usually, he repeats them like a mantra as he speeds toward his own orgasm. Tonight, though, he's reserved them for when I'm able to face him, eye to eye. Chase has saved the profession for when I can witness his absolute candor.

Part of me melts, more happily helpless than when I'd been in the cuffs. I lean forward, brush back the hair that hangs over his ears, and press my lips close. Then I whisper four words, all short and sincere.

He deserves to hear someone say them.

I'm rewarded with a smile and a deep, lingering kiss. He doesn't even notice at first when I roll him over and slip one of the cuffs around his skinny arm, and he certainly doesn't protest when I hook the chain over the much-abused metal bar beneath the padded headboard. His dick springs to life when I confine the other wrist.

"What are you going to do to me now, sir?" He trembles with excitement.

"Don't worry, Son," I say, as I spit onto my fingers and spread the ooze over my hardening dick. "You'll enjoy every moment."

"You'll take care of me?"

With the utmost tenderness, I lift his knees and spread his legs, opening them for my onslaught. "We will take care of each other. I promise."

It's what good dads and sons do, after all.

# THE ARTIST
## BY PETER SCHUTES

✿

I n 1981, The Artist lived in the attic of a massive three-story craftsman-style home in Echo Park. He'd just moved from Northern Europe in search of warmer winters and the aura of happiness, that glittery blanket of stardust and freedom that permeates the air and sparkles on the white sands of Los Angeles' beaches. The Artist had a type. He drew smiling men in tight white t-shirts whose bulging jeans barely covered their full asses, unable to hide the thigh-length erections straining against the denim. Indeed, those erections often sprang forth, creating a tableau of fucking and sucking that glorified the masculine ideal embodied in sex and love between virile men.

Edward, a young cadet in training, met The Artist at the nearby Police Academy coffee shop. He was drawn to The Artist's wise eyes that beheld beauty in authority and order. Edward felt really seen when The Artist gazed at his body. Edward was naturally muscular, with a full ass that strained against his uniform's polyester navy blue slacks. In front, he was so big, his religion showed. He'd asked many times for a looser uniform, but it was against regulations. And so he'd learned to enjoy the envious and admiring stares of his fellow cadets, especially the training officers whose eyes darted below his belt throughout the day.

The physical training was no less forgiving. Edward wore baggy sweats, but they only accentuated the magnificent meat that swung between his legs. He wore a jockstrap, but it couldn't contain him, and eventually, the leg of his sweats would reveal the log-like appendage swaying to and fro as he ran.

Edward's cock wasn't what The Artist noticed first, for he was an ass man, but it clinched the deal. He would pay Edward to model for him. They discussed it over a hamburger and fries tucked away in a corner booth with a view of the many tables of mustached men in uniform. He would pay Edward $40.00, $80.00 if he got it hard and took it out. Edward didn't yet understand why this transaction caused his cock to swell. The thought of this humble, creative man admiring him was intoxicating. He throbbed, unable to stand up when lunch came to an end. He was late for his next class.

Edward lived in an apartment on Laguna, across Sunset from The Artist's place. That Sunday, he climbed a steep set of stairs that led to the palm-lined Laveta Terrace. At the top of the stairs, he could turn and look across at the fountains and paddle boats in Echo Park Lake. It was a crisp, bright December morning. The sunlight reflected off the haze, giving the city a Hollywood-stained dark yellow glow. Uneasy but aroused, Edward adjusted his cock in his jeans before knocking. The Artist's lover answered the door. He was dashingly handsome, with long, sandy-blonde feathered hair and a macho mustache. He extended a hand.

"You must be Edward. I'm Paul. The Artist's out back. Can I get you a coffee?"

Edward shook and smiled. "I'm good. I grabbed a breakfast sandwich at Patra's just now." He gestured behind him. Patra's was a dicey burger joint with more flies than customers.

Paul nodded. "Well, we have antacid for when you need it."

Edward chuckled. "I take it you've eaten there before."

"Yes, unfortunately, I have. Well, come on out back." Paul led Edward through the house. On the walls were pen and ink drawings of men in leather doing things Edward hadn't realized were possible. Huge cocks disappeared into round asses. Lumberjacks choked down each other's meat. It was like a tiny bomb exploded in Edward's brain. He felt ashamed at how much he liked the drawings. But the shame gave way to arousal.

The Artist was in the backyard. A large-format camera sat atop a tripod. The Artist smiled and waved him over to a table piled high with clothing.

"Edward, so glad you could come! You look so handsome, even out of uniform!"

Edward blushed and gave a smile that could knock a queen off her feet. The Artist was no queen; he gave an understated but appreciative grin in return.

Paul helped Edward out of his Derby jacket. The slight chill caused the cadet's nipples to harden against the taut fabric of the white tee, casting shadows in the morning light. As his arms returned to his sides, his muscles rippled. The Artist's eyes widened appreciatively.

Paul nudged The Artist. "You know how to pick them."

The Artist nodded and focused on loading the camera without exposing too much of the film's surface area to the sun. Large-format film was expensive, even in Hollywood.

When Doug held up the leather motorcycle jacket, Edward felt a momentary pang of guilt and pleasure. They'd been studying motorcycle gangs in his class. He knew what the guys who wore those kinds of jackets thought about cops. If a training sergeant saw him wear that jacket, it would be a scandal. But that scandalous edge was exactly what thrilled him about it, too.

The jacket was a perfect fit. The worn leather smelled faintly of cigars and Vaseline. Doug handed Edward a studded leather cap to complete the look.

The Artist gazed down at Edward's K-Swiss sneakers, pursed his lips, and made a tutting sound with his tongue and teeth.

Doug gave Edward a large pair of polished motorcycle boots. They didn't fit right, but he managed to squeeze his size 14 feet into them after several attempts. When Doug stood, dressed head to toe in leather and denim, he was breathtaking. The fact that he didn't see it himself made it all the sexier to the two men admiring him.

The Artist smiled wide, something he almost never did. "Perfect. You are perfect."

"I'll go start the laundry," Doug said, leaving The Artist and his model to work together.

The aroma of the leather jacket was arousing. Edward felt his cock stiffening against his tight jeans as it lengthened and crawled further down his thigh. He absently scratched at the head, tugging on the denim to allow a little more room for his dick. He grinned sheepishly.

Snap! Wind. Snap! The Artist captured those moments of awkward adjustment. He asked Edward to turn away from the camera, pulling his jeans down enough to show the top of his ass crack. Click! Click!

"Please buckle your boot."

Edward put a foot on an upright log and bent over to tighten his shoe. He felt a breeze on the uppermost part of his butt cheeks. The jacarandas swayed in the warm Santa Ana wind. The gentle Los Angeles Winter felt more like Spring.

"Do you wish to make the $80.00?" The Artist asked in a Nordic accent.

Edward nodded. He unbuttoned the top three buttons and reached his hand in, struggling to extract his semi-hard erection from his pant leg. The Artist took three pictures of Edward with his hands down his pants, then one when, at last, the boa constrictor broke out of its cloth cage.

"I must change the film. Please stay hard."

Edward was twenty-two. He'd worked three years in security at the Sherman Oaks Galleria before enlisting as a cadet in the LAPD. He was at that age when merely thinking about sex was enough to keep a man stiff. Up until recently, he could get hard by closing his eyes, picturing pretty girls with big tits holding open their pussies. But today, he thought about the officers and cadets sneaking peeks at his big bulge. He thought about this sensitive artist appreciating him and about the sexy boyfriend, Paul. He thought about those incredible drawings hanging in the house. He was still rock hard when The Artist gave the go-ahead.

Click! Edward held his cock at the balance point, angling it skyward before letting it go. It bobbed and bounced, reflecting the hazy sunshine off the shiny knob. The Artist asked him to take off his jacket and t-shirt, getting shots of him in just his open jeans and those tight boots, his cock protruding from his waist like a panhandle.

"Please lower the jeans so I can see the crack." The Artist pointed to Edward's bulbous butt.

Edward obeyed. The Artist took more shots highlighting the handsome cadet's muscular bottom. Edward tuned into The Artist's admiration like a radio signal. It caused his cock to swell to full mast.

For the final few shots, he pushed the jeans down around his ankles, and then it was a wrap. The Artist gave Edward his money, and they exchanged a cold, formal hug.

❧

Since the house was close to the Academy, Edward decided to head over to the Rifle Club, where the gymnasium and swimming pool were open 24 hours a day. He thought the walk would help alleviate the throbbing hard-on that demanded his attention. It did. The steep descent and subsequent climb to the Academy grounds gave his boner a rest. Blood flowed to leg and thigh muscles instead, giving his cock a chance to deflate.

The Rifle Club was an old building with a heated outdoor pool, a rifle range, and a weight training facility. The place was busy during the week, but on weekends, Edward sometimes had the whole place to himself.

When Edward got to the locker room, he smacked his forehead; he'd forgotten any kind of workout clothes. New sweat pants were eight dollars, money better spent on a few burgers. The Rifle Club wasn't just for cadets and training officers. Any LAPD officer was automatically enrolled as a member.

"Forget something?" A deep, friendly voice called out from the second row of lockers. Edward smiled. He looked down the next row and saw the owner of the voice. It belonged to a man who was probably old enough to retire with a full pension. Wearing only his towel, he looked to be about fifty. Despite his advancing years, the man was buff. His bulging, veiny arms hung from broad, sculpted shoulders. A furry chest of graying hairs ran in a pattern down to his waist, where it disappeared under the towel. Time had been kind to his face. There were crows' feet, but only when he smiled broadly, as he was doing just then.

"Yeah, man, I was gonna work out, but I got all the way here and realized I didn't have my sweats."

"Mark." The man extended a hand.

"Edward." They shook.

"Look, Edward, I worked out pretty hard, but I can loan you my sweats if you don't mind a little perspiration. We look pretty close in size."

Then Edward caught it. That little millisecond where Mark's eyes darted below the waist, briefly raising the lids before coolly returning to gaze at his face. Then again, like a non-verbal, split-second double-take.

Mark said, "Well, at least the same waist size. You look like you might be packing a lot more than me."

Nobody had ever been quite that direct with Edward since high school. There, they called him "Mr. Ed." They jeered and called out "Wi-I-I-bur!" stamping their feet and whinnying. But here at the academy, men never talked about his dick. It was the elephant in the locker room.

"Sorry," Mark said, "I guess that was out of line. Do you want the sweats?"

Edward shrugged. "Yeah, that would be awesome. And yeah, I think I can make it fit." He playfully squeezed his cock through his jeans. Mark grinned appreciatively.

"I'll bet you get a lot of ladies with that thing."

Edward said, "Lots of comers, not many takers." In truth, Edward had never made it with a girl. He got tired of the rejection and preferred taking care of business himself. Literally every girl who'd ever been with him long enough to get naked had backed out.

Mark said, "Why is that?"

Edward was intrigued by this cop taking such interest in his manhood. It was the same feeling he got when The Artist admired his physique. Edward had never been rejected by a guy, but only because he'd never been with one. The gears in the back of his head started shifting and engaging.

Edward said, "There's such a thing as too big."

Then Mark made a bold move. He stepped forward, putting his hand on Edward's crotch. "I'll be the judge of that."

Instantly, Edward's cock sprung to life. Mark massaged it through the denim, gasping softly when it tripled in girth and doubled in length.

Edward had just spent the morning posing nude for another man. It didn't make him gay. But the feeling he got when Mark's fatherly hand landed on his crotch could only be queer.

"Yeah, you like that big boy? You want Daddy to suck you off, son?"

Edward's gut response was to push the man away, but something stronger, more urgent, kept him frozen in place, letting the older man feel him up. He looked down and saw a growing wet spot near the knee of his pant leg, where the tip of his cock oozed excitedly.

Mark followed Edward's gaze, kneeling, putting his

mustached mouth over the damp spot, making it wet with his tongue. Edward had gotten this far with a couple of girls, but it had never excited him like this.

"What if somebody sees us?"

Mark stood and reached into his locker, grabbing a small zippered pouch. "Follow me."

The swarthy older man led Edward to the steam room, which was shut off for the weekend. The door was unlocked, and the only light that came into the room was through the glass. They could see one another, but they were cloaked in darkness to any passersby. Mark clicked the deadbolt, sealing them in.

Mark emptied the pouch. He had a mini-tub of Vaseline and a small, dark brown bottle. He opened the bottle and sniffed.

"Here." He held the bottle up to Edward's nose. It smelled like an explosion at an airplane glue factory. His head immediately began swimming. Mark squatted, fumbling and fussing with the buttons of Edward's jeans, then down they came. Edward's cock sprang out hard, smacking Mark with a loud uppercut to the jaw.

Mark fell on his ass, laughing. "Holy shit! Ed! That's one motherfucking huge dong you got!"

But it didn't sound angry or afraid, like when the girls said it. This was an appreciative compliment—a total turn-on.

Mark added, "This is gonna be hard work."

Again, this was said with conviction, not exasperation. Mark wasn't going to back down. Edward felt hope like never before. Was he going to lose his virginity?

"It won't fit in your mouth, will it?"

Mark laughed. "My mouth? No." He dipped three fingers in the Vaseline. With both hands, he spread the glob up and down the length of Edward's throbbing cock. Edward's eyes rolled up in his head. No girl had ever gone this far with him. He was used to doing it for himself. He sucked air through the gap in his front teeth.

Mark dipped again, but this time he put the Vaseline between his butt cheeks. Ed watched Mark's fingers disappear into the hole. One, then two. Then three and four. He got the thumb in and stretched until his whole hand and wrist snapped past the tight rectum. He pulled out a clenched fist, forming a gape. With his greasy hand, he stroked the head of Edward's cock, then brought it to his hole, where Edward felt, for the first time, that soft embrace of someone else's quivering flesh around his own. It was only the very tip, resting against the hole.

Mark inhaled from the brown bottle. Holding and guiding Edward's dick, he pressed back, letting a half inch of the enormous cock head slip inside. Edward had to think about his ugly Sunday School teacher, Ms. Clark, in order to keep from coming that instant.

"Oh, Jesus!" Mark's body trembled as it struggled to accommodate Edward's massive member. He inhaled another whiff of the bottle and eased back, letting in another half inch. Then, in a show of brute strength, Mark pressed with great effort until suddenly, there was an audible pop. The head was inside. Edward's corona was relatively large compared to his shaft. Once the mushroom head was past the gate, it took Mark only seconds to fill his rectum with Edward's flesh. With one leg planted in front, Mark rocked his hips to and fro, stroking Edward's cock with his anus.

"Wait! Oh shit! I'm gonna come."

Mark sped up. "Do it. I need your special sauce if we're gonna fry this burger up right."

Edward couldn't hold back the flood. Though it had only been a day or two, it felt like a year's worth of come flooded Mark's ass. It began to squirt out past Edward's cock, running down the two men's thighs and splashing on the tile floor of the steam room. Edward was too turned on to lose his hard-on. He throbbed inside the older man, fermenting in his juices.

Mark said, "Now we're ready. Watch this, son."

Lifting one leg and twisting, Mark pressed hard until it seemed there was nowhere else for Edward to go. Then as if he'd torn a hole in the man, his cock pressed further, slipping through a second tight hole up inside.

Mark pounded the tile wall. "Ngggh! Ahhhr! Oh, god, there it goes. There it goes."

Then Mark's firm, hard butt tickled Edward's pubes as it pressed against him. They were locked together, Edward buried deep inside his older companion.

"You ever been in the second hole, boy?"

"N-no-no sir. I've never been in a hole."

"I spoiled you for all the men to come, then. They're gonna have to learn how to let you in."

Without even coming close to slipping out, Edward held Mark by the waist as he sat down. The older man rotated so he was facing his impaler. He leaned in for a kiss. It caused Edward to swell even larger. Until that day, modeling for The Artist, then in that moment he met Mark, he never knew he wanted to be with a man. A manly man, with fur and gray: a daddy. Now he was belly-button deep inside a daddy, and he never wanted to leave. As if to prove how deep he was, Mark bounced and pointed to a lump in his gut.

"See that, Ed, that's you."

Mark held onto Edward's back and shoulders as leverage while he rose and sat repeatedly, stroking the huge cock with his insides. Edward had tried to get this feeling before, wrapping his cock in a greased leather chamois wedged between his mattress and box spring, but it felt nothing like being inside a warm, furry daddy. His previous cum sloshed inside the man's guts, making slurping sounds as he slid up and down the massive pole.

Edward felt a slipperiness on his tummy. He looked

down and saw Mark's big daddy dick leaking a snail-trail of juice on his abdomen.

"You see that, stud? You're pushing that right out of me." Mark dipped a finger in it and fed it to Edward. It tasted sweet. The older man put his feet on the bench astride Edward's waist and leaned back with his hands on the cadet's knees. He formed a bridge, thrusting upward and sitting back down. Edward could feel another orgasm building. He watched Mark's hard cock rising and falling as he impaled himself with bridge thrusts.

Mark said, "Put it in your mouth." He stopped thrusting, holding in a reverse bridge, his fat dick waving in front of Edward's face.

It was a day of many firsts. Edward inclined his head and put Mark in his mouth. It was big, but not huge. It was easy. Mark began riding up and down, his cock sliding in and out of Edward's mouth. It smelled like Aqua Velva and tasted like popcorn. The buttery precum coated his tongue, causing him to drool.

Mark clamped his ass cheeks hard around Edward's dick, making the strokes twice as intense. Thrusting up and down, he said, "I'm close, son. You want Daddy's load in your mouth?"

"Mmmhmm." He did. He wanted it, no matter how wrong he used to think that would be. He wanted to suck and swallow. He was hungry for cum.

Mark's balls drew up tight. "Here it comes." A rich flow of hot, salty brew gurgled into Edward's greedy mouth. He gulped, wanting more, until Mark was spent.

Mark said, "Now it's time you work for your supper."

He stood, letting Edward's towering cock break free from his ass. He lay on the bench.

"Fuck me, son."

Edward marveled at the loose hole between Mark's ass cheeks. It hung like a pouty pair of lips in an anal frown. He pushed past the opening easily, sliding up inside until he reached the back wall. The daddy shifted until, with a snap, the cadet went deep into his colon.

Edward snorted hot air through his nostrils as he began thrusting, then picked up the pace. His thighs smacked into Mark's ass, making a clapping sound. Mark lifted the brown bottle to his nose and inhaled.

"You want some?" He held it to Edward's nostril, not really offering him a choice. He inhaled, and the room spun. He kept thrusting, his legs trembling as he struggled to stay on his feet.

"Yeah, fuck your daddy, boy. Fuck him!"

Edward obeyed. He held the man by the waist to keep from pushing him along the tile bench. Both men were sweating as if the steam room had been switched on, but it was just their own heat and passion. The room filled with the odors of the older and younger man, the poppers, the mildew under the tile, and that unique aroma of anal sex.

Edward watched fascinated as the outline of his cock moved beneath the taut skin of the older man's belly. He pressed and felt the pressure on the corona as he slipped past.

Mark was hard again, jacking himself off while Edward pounded him. Edward watched enviously as the man was able to completely encircle his cock with one hand, cupping his balls with the other. Edward needed both hands on his cock. Even then, his fingers couldn't touch. In his mind's eye, he merged his fucking with Mark's self-stroking, until he was jacking himself with the smaller dick. It brought him close. He leaned forward and took a lick from the tip of the older man's cock.

"Oh, yeah. You want another load? You hungry?"

Edward nodded. Mark jacked himself furiously. Not wanting to lose the illusion, Edward fucked harder and faster, still imagining his cock the mere above-average size of the older man.

"Oh yeah, fuck, rip me a new one!" Mark bucked

and jerked, his face reddening with the effort of withstanding the rough fuck from his younger companion.

"Oh shit. Oh, here, come get it." Mark jerked furiously, his body bucking, as another load escaped his cock. Edward clamped his mouth over the head, sucking down the creamy load as it spilled from Mark's slit.

The taste and smell were too much. Edward felt a churning in his balls.

Mark said, "Oh, you ready to give Daddy another load? You ready, son?"

Edward didn't answer, distracted by the flood of fantasies and sensations that battled for his attention. He just kept thrusting, savoring the cum in his mouth, letting the older man's flesh funnel encircle his cock. He was inside one of The Artist's drawings, drowning in male pleasure.

"Come on son, give your Daddy your cum!"

Clamping his hands on Mark's thighs, he pulled the man closer with each thrust. Mark put his ankles over Edward's big shoulders so that he could lean into him. Edward's massive upper body pressed until Mark's knees bent towards his ears. He folded like a paper clip.

Seeing Mark so vulnerable, he felt powerful. His tremendous cock plugged the man over and over. Edward's hips sped to a blur. Mark's eyes fluttered and rolled.

"Fuck your daddy! Fuck your daddy!" Mark absently reached up and pinched Edward's meaty nipple.

That was a switch Edward never knew about. It was sudden, like turning on the garbage disposal in the middle of the night. He jumped, astonished. Mark grabbed both nipples, twisting and tugging. It was all Edward needed.

"Fuck, I'm coming." In giant spurts, the young cadet unloaded himself deep inside the older cop. They stayed together, gasping heavily as if they'd just completed a calisthenics class.

"So, cadet, do you still need to borrow those sweats?"

Edward grinned. "Nope."

❧

THAT THURSDAY, THE ARTIST PHONED EDWARD AND told him the drawing was done. He climbed the concrete steps to Laveta Terrace, wondering what it would look like.

Doug answered the door. "Edward! Come in. I don't know if The Artist told you, but he often photographs models separately and draws them together. The other model's here for the unveiling, too. The Artist drew you two together. It's beautiful. Come see"

Edward stopped short when he saw Mark in the dining room talking to The Artist. Mark looked up, just as surprised.

The Artist said, "You two know each other from the Academy, yeah?" He unveiled the graphite drawing. Edward's bare biker ass reflected the sun as he stuck his massive cock into Mark's muscled cop hole.

"I call it 'The Bad Boy and the Daddy Cop.' What do you think?"

❧

# TUXES N' TAILS

## BY CHUCK IDGAF

# SATURDAY

Hi. My name is Chris. When I was 19, almost 20, I worked at a tuxedo shop while in college. This was a confusing time in my life. Given my upbringing, I wasn't near ready to admit I was attracted to men. I had been a total geek in high school, with no social life. However, I was coming into my own in college, finding my tribe, at least from a hobbies and interests standpoint. I was still trying to date girls at school, although very awkwardly. I even experimented sexually with two of them. But all my fantasies were of men. And I mean men. Not other college boys. Middle-aged men. Preferably with a nice pot belly and covered in manly hair front and back. But as a young man, anything sexual, no matter the gender or genitalia, was going to get me going pretty good. This and my lack of attraction to what Hollywood had shown me are typical homosexuals likely added to my confusion about my sexuality. So that's a bit of the step up. Let me take you back in time to a story I hope you'll enjoy.

⚜

I've worked at the tuxedo shop for almost a year. It's better than working retail at the mall. You can make commissions from sales, and booking wedding parties. I'm just getting trained on booking weddings and all the upselling, etc., but the job mainly involves fittings for tux rentals and all the work in the back getting the tuxes ready each week.


IT'S SATURDAY, AND I'M SCHEDULED TO OPEN. I PULL into the lot at the strip mall and notice the owner's van is there. I think that's weird until I remember the manager is on vacation. Jon, the owner, usually works a regular day shift, meaning I only see him in passing when I come in on weekday evenings after class. He's a really nice guy, lots of dad jokes, though. He takes owning the business seriously, and his approach with his employees is more like family. He teaches us the right way to do things (or at least his preferred way), uses positive reinforcement, and never says anything negative or condescending.

I rattle the door, which is what most of us usually do to let someone in the back know to let us in. I wait a few minutes and try again...and again. Finally, Jon comes around the corner. He's a bit flustered looking—not mad, rushed, maybe. He unlocks the door and holds it open for me.

"Sorry about that; I was in the 'john,'" putting a little emphasis on 'john' because it could be a delicate subject matter. I think to myself, it's funny that he's so proper.

"We all gotta go," I say. Since only about five minutes are left before he opens the store, I add, "I should probably do that before you open."

"Good idea," he says, "It's just us until about 1:00."

Jon follows me to the back. I clock in while he's getting the money drawer together. I take a peek at how far last night's crew got on starting production for next week. With what's left in the store, you can only do so much on the weekend, but it needs to be done. They didn't even get started. I'm guessing it was a lot of last-minute pickups the night before. Jon goes out to load up the register and open the door. So I go to piss before I start. There's a single bathroom built into the back room of the store. Clearly, an afterthought, the way it's slapped together. The light switch is on the far wall, closer to the toilet, instead of inside the door by the sink. Most of us leave the door open so we can find the switch, then close it. I don't know why, maybe I had to go worse than I thought, or perhaps it's just too early on a Saturday, but I flipped the switch and started to piss without closing the door.

I'm almost done, and I look down and notice a magazine open on the sink, a dirty magazine, and I'm not talking about Playboy. This woman had huge fake tits and a dildo closer to a traffic cone she is squatting over while rubbing herself and making a wild face. It's a good thing I was almost done pissing because my stream stopped as my erection started. I flipped through a few pages. The first few were all part of the same lady in various poses. The next set is a Swedish yodeler costume. I stopped flipping when I got to the third set in the magazine. It was a typical college co-ed type kneeling, looking up with mouth open at one of the two men standing on each side of her, slightly behind her, all facing the camera. The men were cut off just above the belly button. One had a slight paunch with a slight, chestnut happy trail, a four-inch soft cock with an extra inch of foreskin hanging over the tip under a thick bush. The other had a bit of a potbelly covered in black curly fur. His soft cock was like mine in that it was mostly just a head sitting on top of his balls. However, unlike mine, his head was an impossibly thick knob, and his full tight scrotum was the size of a softball. The title for the set was "Old Men, Young Woman."

I'm standing there awkwardly with my dick out, still pointing at the toilet while my torso is turned so I can flip the magazine on the sink. I'm so captivated seeing images of the men and my mind already thinking how I'd give anything to swap with the woman in the picture that I don't hear a quick shuffle of shoe soles running through the back room. I'm mid-page-flip and get just a glimpse of both men, hard and her, about to blow the thinner one, when Jon reaches the door. I drop the page in shock (without getting a good look at the details I wanted). Jon says, "I'm sorry. I'm so sorry." He grabs the magazine and turns away. I realize my not-quick 6-inch boner is sticking out. I sort of get it wedged in my pants going left and zip up. Jon moves to give me room to come out of the bathroom. He turns towards me, bright red in the face.

I've always thought Jon was attractive, even if a little thinner than my fantasies normally. He's maybe 40, I guess. Tall. I'm 6'2". He's like 6'6" at least. Slim, maybe just a bit of a paunch, but hard to tell with a tucked-in dress shirt that's slightly pulled out. He's got a full head of chestnut hair, but his beard has a definite dark red hue to it with just a few grey hairs starting to show.. He hasn't buttoned his top shirt button yet or snugged up his tie, and I can see a nice thick patch of even darker red/brown hair on his chest.

"I'm so sorry. That was so inappropriate of me to have this here," he says as he clutches the magazine to his chest, trying to hide it.

"It's ok, Jon. We all do it."

He starts to smile and respond, but multiple chimes cut him off from customers coming in the door. He looks towards the opening leading out front from where we are in the back. The owner of the business clearly takes over his mind and body as he turns back towards me and gives me the nod to follow him out front. He quickly throws the magazine in his briefcase as I pass him heading to the front. I haven't even fin-ished saying "How can I help you?" when he arrives be-side me. It's a large wedding party here to register AND be fitted for a wedding less than a month away. We give each other a look because we all feel the same way about last-minute people. I start to get my stuff for the fittings when he hands me the wedding book. I look at him like 'What are you doing?', assuming he'll book it. He says, "I've heard you're ready. And I'm here to double-check your first one on your own." I think it's nice, but I also slightly wonder if it's because of what just happened.

҉

I FINISHED BEFORE HE FITTED EVERYONE AND HELPED with the last few. Jon had looked over my work while the guys were in the dressing rooms. He complimented me on my delivery style with the customers, plus they wanted fancy tuxes, AND I upsold a bunch of accessories because they wanted 'fancy'. It'll be a nice commission. I was kind of proud I'd impressed the owner. I think he wanted to break it down some more and give me some pointers, but another group walked in, returning from a Friday night event. We got them all checked in together, which I don't think Jon does a lot anymore, since he usually doesn't work on weekends. But it was nice to see he's not above doing any job in the place he owns.

҉

WE GOT ALL THE RETURNS TO THE BACK AND STARTED breaking them down to go to the cleaners and put up the bits that don't like cufflinks. We were just working in silence. I looked over to see that Jon was a little red-faced again. He caught me looking, and he got redder.

"You ok?" I ask.

"I'm just kind of embarrassed," he says.

"Why? Because you were having a tug before anyone got here?"

He stifles a guffaw at my bluntness, then nods, still embarrassed.

"Like I said, we all do it," I pause. "Is it because I

59

know what you were doing or because of why I think you were doing it?" It was a bold question, but I was curious.

He finally looks up from where he's been staring down at the floor. "Mostly because you know I was doing it. Although you are right, most men do…but now I'm not sure what to say since you brought up why I was doing it."

"Bluntly, I'm just assuming because you don't get enough at home. No offense."

He nodded. He made a sheepish face and mumbled, "Understatement."

"Yeah," I say, "I overheard my dad complain about that a lot over the years to his buddies. I kind of figure it's a common problem."

Jon nods.

I feel like being bold, "So can I ask why here, not at home?"

The redness in his face has almost faded away. He shrugs. "My wife and kids are always around. I can sometimes sneak one late at night in the bathroom, but I have to get up early to get here anyway. Easier to come in here alone and enjoy my 'literature' without fear of interruption."

"Never thought about that. I guess I also have a tough time finding privacy at home, now that I think about it. Thanks for the honesty. And, uh, sorry you saw my penis."

He laughs loudly. I think it was the tension breaker he needed. "Well, we've all seen one," he says to me in the same way I said "We all do it" earlier.

Now I'm embarrassed and flushed, and I kind of shake my head.

He says, "Wait. You've never seen another naked man? Like in a locker room or anything."

I reply, "Well, I've seen my dad get out of the shower soft. Once, when I was little, I walked in on them fooling around because I'd thrown up in the bed, but it was dark."

Jon laughs.

"I was a band geek; I never took gym at school. Never been in any locker room."

"So everyone is naked in the locker room?" I ask. "That was always one of my fears, popping a bone in front of everyone." I add, mumbling, "And worrying about being smaller."

His tone of voice turns warm, trying to comfort me, "Those are common concerns, especially in your teens. I played sports in college, so it was pretty common to see nudity, but not everyone. Also, I think a lot of guys like to compare themselves to others, so there's definitely some peeking going on."

'Really," I ask, now embarrassed but oddly comfortable talking to Jon. "I always wonder because I feel like I'm kind of small, at least compared to my dad."

Jon pauses, clearly thinking if he should say anything. "I wasn't looking on purpose and didn't get a good look, but it looked pretty average from the flash, I remember."

I give him a thankful nod. That was a kind thing to say.

My curiosity still piqued, I eventually asked, "So... some of the guys in the locker room were hard?"

"Sure. Don't you get random boners?"

"All the time," I say with a bit of how awkward they still are to hide, especially since I'm trying to hide one now.

"I mean, there were a few guys who would openly jerk off in the shower later at night when no one was around."

"Really?" I ask, incredulous at the idea.

"Sure," Jon says. "Some guys do it 3, 4, 5 times a day. You've got to fit those in the schedule when you can."

"Wow," I say, "I mean, I do it most days. But I can usually only cum once." I flush when I say the word before I think about it. "I mean it will get hard again, but then when I've tried for a 2nd time, I either rub myself raw or the one time I managed to get to what should have been a climax, it was more like a slightly painfully penile dry heave."

Jon says, "Interesting. In my youth, I could do it two or three times every day and often would. Hell, if I had the house to myself, I probably still could most days." He laughs.

"Do you do it every day?" I ask, quickly adding, "My bad, that's none of my business."

"It's ok. Just don't tell anyone." He winks. "Most of the weekdays I come in early to cum early, if you catch my drift." He chuckles.

I roll my eyes. He always makes lame jokes. But I laugh a little because it's kind of funny. Also impressed he's got that kind of sex drive and a bit jealous he can cum more than once in a day.

Unfortunately, the door chime rings from more customers. Other employees arrive soon after that. I would have liked to continue the conversation. But the rest of the day was fairly busy, so my mind didn't linger. And the large wet spot in my tighty-whities finally dries after about an hour. I did have an incredible orgasm that night in bed, thinking about those men in the magazine.

# 2

# SUNDAY

I t's Sunday morning. My parents have always been sticklers about church. Even though I'm in community college, I still live at home. However, I have to be at work about the time the service is over. Walking out would be rude, so I just skip it after Sunday School, get breakfast at a drive-thru, and eat in the parking lot, listening to mixtapes while I wait on the manager to show up and open the store. This gives me some downtime and is a nice occasional Sunday ritual for "me time." The drive-through was fast, so I've got just more than an hour before we open.

I HAVEN'T BEEN THERE LONG, JUST FINISHING MY biscuit sandwich, when Jon, in typical style, pulls up way earlier than the manager would. He exits the car and waves his arm, signaling me to "come on in" while walking to the door. I get to the door just as he finishes fumbling with his giant ring of keys and is getting the door unlocked. "It's just us today. Becky called in sick. Fortunately, we left the place pretty ready to go last night, so we've got some time to kill before we open." He winks at me. My cock jumps. I don't think he means anything, but my dick doesn't know that.

As he locks the door, Jon says, "I'll get the register

loaded. Then, we can handle things in the back until we open. I'll take the front today with returns, and you can focus on breakdowns. There are a fair amount of returns scheduled today. I'll call if I need help with some fittings."

"Sounds like a good plan, so we don't get behind," I say.

I start back on the production line, and Jon prepares the store's front. We've still got more than an hour before we open because he came in so early. Missing my downtime, I think, "Better to be on the clock, though." Jon finishes a few things at his desk that's kind of hidden in the corner down the first row of hanging racks. But I can hear he's not seated. More like pacing in place. He's usually sitting while he works. I'm around the corner pulling shirts for next week's production line. It occurs to me that he may have had other plans coming in so early. I muster up the courage to say, "Uh...don't let me interrupt your routine." I put a little emphasis on "routine". He laughs and walks around the corner.

"How about my turn to ask you some personal questions?"

I blush at his statement. I nod. "Fair is fair," I say.

"Are you dating? Have you gotten any yet?" he emphasizes 'gotten any.'

"Wow," I say, "I guess I deserve that." I laugh. "I was seeing a girl last summer before she went out-of-state to school. She gave me some blow jobs, and I went down on her some."

"That's great, man," he says with pride. "Plus, you don't have to worry about getting pregnant."

"Bonus," I say.

Jon cocks his head like he's thinking before asking, "So your locker room questions got me thinking; you've never been in a circle jerk. You know what that is, right?"

I nod. "I've heard of it, but I didn't think that was a real thing."

"Sure," Jon says. "Full disclosure. I was one of those guys in the showers late at night that I was talking about." He chuckles. "But I wasn't alone in taking advantage of the empty space. There were a few of us. Either I walked in on them or vice versa. Most guys would try to hide it or get embarrassed, finish showering, and leave. But a few of us would continue until climax. If I walked in and they continued, I'd join in my stall. If they walked in on me and started jerking, I'd turn to face them. We'd often watch each other. There were about 8 guys, including me. We eventually organized. Called ourselves Bate Bros. 5 of us were pretty much daily. The others joined occasionally. It was an open shower room with showers around the outer wall. We'd all stand in our stall, facing in, and watch each other. We started getting verbal. Encouraging each other to stroke, to shoot. We'd sometimes have contests to see who could shoot the farthest. I'd usually win." He winks with a smile. "Harmless fun. And good male bonding."

I'm breathless. My not-quite 6-inch cock curves a little to the left, so fortunately, my erection had grown that way during his story and wasn't painfully bound up in my briefs. I'm sure my wet spot will soak through my pants soon. If I'm not mistaken, I think Jon's cock is straining against this underwear, still tucked in a downward position.

"That...sounds...amazing." I manage to hoarsely get out finally. "I hope I could stumble into an experience like that someday."

Jon raises his eyebrows and nods slowly. "Well," he shrugs.

I thought I'd cum without touching myself.

"Are you...offering?" I ask. I'm almost shaking.

"If you're cool with it. I'm not looking for any trouble. I'm taking a risk since you work for me. But I'd love a trip down memory lane if we can shake on it, like men, that it's just good old-fashioned male bonding. Those were some fun experiences.

"Su-Su-Sure." I stutter. We shake on it.

He goes to his briefcase. "I miss those guys from college. We really bonded and became friends. We'd hang out socially, too. But we all lost touch after graduation, getting married, and having kids, and such. Man, I need a social life." He chuckles at his own thoughts." He pulls a different magazine and a bottle of lotion from the briefcase.

As we walk over to the open space of the workroom, showing me the bottle of lotion. He says, "You mentioned rubbing yourself raw. You need a good lube. Since neither of us lives alone, a proper lube is hard to hide. They are much better than this, but this works pretty well. This is Corn Huskers Lotion. You can get it most places. It doesn't dry up too fast, but if it starts to get sticky, you can just spit on it a little. It also washes up easily. And you can just say it's for your dry feet if someone finds it."

I nod, impressed with the info.

"Now I'm usually good with a dry stroke for my first one of the day. Sounds like you are, too. But get some kind of lube, and you might be able to pull off a second load sometime." He smiles kindly at me. I feel a kind of warmth, realizing he's a mentor of sorts. He sets the lotion off to the side.

"I noticed what page you were on the other day and thought we might be into some of the same scenarios, so I brought another magazine today."

My stomach flips. I know my eyes are probably wide with fright.

He lays down the magazine on the big table in the middle of the workroom, and I try to stifle a sigh of relief. It's called "Hot Babes and Sugar Daddies." There's a topless young woman sitting in the lap of a silver-haired man in a suit with a big mustache and a cigar. I smirk and nod, thinking about the mustache wrapped around my cock.

"I thought so," and playfully jabs me in the arm. "I like imaging when I'm older that I could pull some hot, young co-eds. Hell, if I wasn't married, I'd like to pull some now." He chuckles at himself. I let out a little laugh.

He starts to flip through the magazine. With his other hand, he's rubbing his cock through his pants. It appears to still be held downward by his briefs. I'm lightly rubbing mine, still pointing left in my pants.

The first set of photos is related to the cover photo. The woman is nude now. The series of photos include the man blowing cigar smoke on her privates, a few un-sanitary things with the cigar, and then a thick cock through the fly of the man's suit.

"Oh yeah," Jon says. "Look at her suck that thick thing." He continues to flip pages, pausing a bit on each one.

The next set is an older man, smooth, with a pretty big belly that catches my attention a little. He's got amazing big nipples. I start to stroke as best I can through my pants, looking at them. The girl in this set is a "nurse" giving him a sponge bath.

I hear Jon unzip his pants. "Yeah, I'd love her to bathe me like that." He's reaching into his fly. I'm trying to look at the magazine and not over at Jon. I can tell in my peripheral vision that he's adjusted his cock upward and is rubbing it through his underwear.

I can't take it. I unzip and pull my briefs under my balls, pulling my cock and balls out through my fly as he flips the page. The old man in the photos is bent over, with the woman playing with his butthole and washing his huge, dangly balls. I'm thinking about licking and playing with those big balls.

Jon turns to me, "Do you know about prostate mas-sage?" I shake my head. "I'll tell you some other time," he says as he turns back to the magazine.

Jon flips to the next page. It's the beginning of a new set of photos. My jaw drops. The woman is on all fours, her ass and privates towards the camera. The man in front of her, I assume, about to get a blow job, is a sexy professor type. Grey temples, dark hairy torso, slender, a normal-looking cock, a little bigger than mine, maybe 6 inches and about the same thickness. The man behind her looks like he's stepping up to mount her, but still turned partially towards the camera, is more of a football coach type. Salt and pepper mustache and hair, but balding on top. A nice pot belly, not too big. Covered in thick, long fur. Front, back, sides, shoulders, arms. Silver towards the chest, but still darker on the belly and bush. His cock is uncut, with just the crown of the head exposed. Fat and veiny, but also about 6 inches like the other man.

I start to stroke furiously. "Hell yeah. Stroke it, man. I knew we had similar tastes. The thought of her getting double-teamed really gets me going," Jon says while looking at the page.

I'm pretty sure we're looking at different things in the picture, but I don't care. I look over at him, smile, and nod. He smiles and winks back. I can see out of the corner of my eye without looking down he has both hands at his fly now like he's trying to get his cock out. I can see a bit of the waistband, similar to my tighty-whities. As I start to turn back to the magazine, I can't help but look down a little just as he's pulling out his cock. I did a double-take to confirm what I saw. I stop stroking, slack-jawed. He notices that I've stopped, and I'm looking directly at his boner.

"Yeah. I'm not huge, but a little above average," he says. It's at least 7 inches, maybe closer to 8. Rigid hard. Not slim, but not thick. Maybe like a roll of quarters. It's got a slight downward bend, which explains how it wasn't killing him trapped in those briefs earlier. It occurs to me that when he flipped it up, his head was clearly above his waistband, and he was playing with the sensitive part under the head. That's an area I like to concentrate on, too. He's got his balls still inside his briefs, so I can't see them. But a bit of bush is peeking out, and it's even redder than his beard.

I just nod at his comment about "a little above average" and think it's quite a bit more than mine. I turn and go back to stroking.

"Yeah, I'd love to spitroast a chick with a buddy one day," Jon says. His tone is different like the horniness is taking over. "I bet she'd love it." He continues, "I wonder which hole that guy with the fat one is going for? I'd love to try anal sometime. I hear it's so tight, it just squeezes the cum right out of you."

Jon flips to the next page. Both men are inside her now in this photo. "Looks like I guessed wrong," he says, "but, man, look how stretched she is by that fat cock."

I manage an "uh-huh" as I focus on the veins in what's left exposed on the man's shaft and the back hair you can see even better in this photo. Then looking towards the other man in the photo, who is pulling both his nipples as she sucks him.

Jon's really getting verbal now, with an animalistic quality to his voice. He's thrusting his hips a little as he strokes. "I like my long shaft, but I wouldn't mind having a thick hog to stretch out some lips." He continues in a bit," My cunt wife complains it's too long and I jab her on a full stroke. I can't be gentle all the time. Sometimes I just want to plow." His strokes become more frantic.

Jon is staring at the woman being spit-roasted. I look over at his cock, only moving my eyes, not my head. It's slick around the head with precum. I wonder how it tastes. My mouth is dry thinking about having Jon's cock in it.

He turns the page. The woman is on her back. The "professor" straddles her chest, holding her head with his cock in her mouth. I can now see the full upper body of the "coach". I want to straddle his furry belly and shoot my load into his thick fur while twisting his big nipples.

Jon's almost yelling at the magazine, "Yeah buddy. Skull fuck that bitch. Make her gag on your cock. Yeah. Make her take it all. "Fuuuuckkk" Jon's head pitches back. I turn just in time to clearly see his first volley of cum shoot out.

I'm used to mine, which dribbles out in ¼ and ½ teaspoon-sized spurts over maybe 3 good contractions. Jon's is a thick, inches-long stream that hits the wall a good 10 feet on the other side of the room. The second hit the far end of the 8-foot table we're standing at. He grunts louder with each spasm. The third just clears the magazine. Grunts 4-8 more fall to the floor, each spurt more cum than my typical load. His eyes are still closed, but his head is still back. His cock is slowly softening. I turn back to the magazine. I flip the page. It's coach in full glory, pulled out cumming on her belly. I look at the skin pulled back on his veiny shaft, exposing his shiny head. His sweaty fur clumped up. I stroked harder and faster, thinking about it being me laying there.

Softer now, Jon says, "Yeah, buddy. Stroke it. Think about all those dirty things you want to do. Think about all those dirty things you want done to you." I imagine it's the "coach" talking to me. Jon continues, "That's it. Stroke that nice cock. Get ready for the plea-sure of shooting your load. The power of your cock. That's it. You can do it. Shoot it for me. Show me that cum. Shoot your load for me, son." The thought of the "coach" in the magazine and Jon both calling me "son" as I stroke sends me over the edge. I begin to shoot my load. I'm not a loud cummer. More of an "unh" and deep breaths. Like normal, my orgasm is 3 good spasms that mostly just fall off the end of my dick into a puddle on the table. It's a bigger load than usual, a bit more than a tablespoon.

Jon pats me on the back. "Nice load, man."

I nod, trying not to look directly at Jon's cock. It's still hanging out his fly, but now about half limp. Unlike mine, I get the feeling his dangles quite a bit even when limp. He turns and walks to the bathroom. He brings me a paper towel to wipe my still drooling cock with. He's already got a paper towel wrapped around his cock with his other hand. He hands me more paper towels from under his arm. I wipe my spunk off the table and his off the floor while he walks around and wipes the other end of the table. Then, he takes the cummerbund from the wall he'd soaked with his first shot of spunk. "I'm sure this has seen worse on a prom night," he laughs, then walks around the corner to put it in the laundry. When he returns, he is all zipped up. I begin to get my now half-hard cock back in my pants.

"Was that ok?" he asks. "I didn't cross any lines or anything?"

"It was great," I reply. I turn a little red. "I liked the 'encouragement.'"

"Great." He claps his hands, back to the carefree, 50s era-dad-next-door personality I'm used to. He looks at his watch. "We should open." Jon turns and walks out front.

# 3

# CLOSING TIME

Fortunately, Sundays are short days. Although there is a steady stream of returns, we keep pace with the work, so there isn't a pile at the end. We closed. Jon is counting down the register and doing all the closing paperwork. I'm trying to finish pulling a few things for the next week's orders. That's pretty typical on Sunday, to do what we can with what's in stock and then just have to deal with what comes back from the cleaners later in the week.

Jon's around the corner at the desk, kind of hidden from view of the workroom. Earlier, I heard him going through drawers and shuffling the reservation book, etc., but nothing much in the last bit. We've been working about 15 minutes or so, and I'm almost done, and know he will be ready to go soon. I hear a strange metal clank from the desk area. It occurred to me that it sounded a bit like a belt buckle. I slow what I'm doing and listen closer. I don't stop completely, knowing he'll notice not hearing the rushing of plastic bags over the clean shirts I'm working with. I go to grab something, but my view is blocked.

On my next pass, I walk around the long way of the large table. The upper rack on the row by the desk was full and blocking most of the view, but the bottom wasn't. I can just see the bottom of the chair he is sitting in. I can also see that his thighs are bare. His pants and tighty-whities are around his ankles. I hang up the stuff in my hands on the rack and make another pass, slower this time, ducking a bit to get a better look. I can't see much more other than his arm blocking my view of his crotch. "Wow," I think. "He wasn't kidding. He's ready to go again."

I guess I'd stopped and stared too long because he said, in a kind but playful voice," You gonna stay over there like a peeping tom, or are you gonna come over here and get a good look at what you'd like to see?"

I swallow the lump in my throat. I hang the stuff in my hand on the rack. As I walk around the corner, He's sitting at the desk, looking at the original magazine from yesterday. His arms are on the chair and still blocking the view, so I can't tell how aroused he is already. I stop a few feet away.

He turns his head to look at me. He smiles softly at me. "I'm so glad we can enjoy the same magazines." He pauses. "But I'm pretty sure we aren't looking at the same things in the pictures."

My heart beats out of my chest. I swallow another dry lump down my throat. I can feel I'm flush and starting to sweat. I can't breathe.

"It's ok," he says. "I'm not gonna judge you. I'm pretty open-minded."

I let out a sigh that's a little too big. I stutter, "Th-th-thanks. Was I...was I that obvious?"

"Well, at the end, earlier, I thought you might be looking at the big furry guy, not the girl on the page." I blushed and kind of turned away. Jon continued, "Plus, I was pretty sure you were looking at my cock a lot longer than just comparing." I look back at him, my eyes wide, thinking I'd hidden it better. Jon says, "Is this what you'd like to see?" he pushes the chair back from the desk and swivels towards me. He slouches a little into the chair as he moves. Laying back a little, sliding his ass closer to the front edge of the seat. His legs are spread, covered in reddish-chestnut hair, his pants and briefs still around his ankles. His shirt is gathered at his waist, fully displaying his much redder bush. His cock is at full mast, standing straight up into the air. It looks even bigger than it did, poking out of this fly. I just stare at it. My mouth is somehow watering and dry at the same time. I just slowly nod in response to his question.

"You can take a better look. I don't mind. I don't think any man should have any shame in front of another." I take a few steps forward. The head to his circumcision scar is light pink. The skin is pale and fair-skinned, with a couple of bulging blue veins. I finally snap out of being mesmerized by his cock and notice his balls, not big, kind of the low end of medium, like mine, but boy does his sack hang. They are just over the front of the chair seat. If he were to sit on the edge of the seat, they'd probably hang four to six inches. "Do you like what you see?" he asks.

I look him in the eye. I softly manage to say, "Yes."

"Would you be interested in a mutually beneficial arrangement?" he asks with a devilish smirk.

I look at him a little confused, not clear exactly what he's saying.

Jon chuckles a little. "I'm into women. But I'm also into getting off. Seems like...you've got some things to figure out. Understand?"

I nod, saying, "Yes. I think."

"Clearly, you've got some exploring you'd like to do. Do you see how that could be mutually beneficial?"

"Sure." I nod again, starting to get the idea.

"So...in that case. What would you like to do, Chris?"

I stare like a deer in headlights.

"Would you like to play with my cock?" he jokingly prods.

"Yes, sir." I barely get out, my mouth so dry from nerves.

"I'm ok with that," he says in a kind voice. "I might look at my magazine some, no offense. What would you like to do?"

"Uh...." I stammer, "Suck it?" More of a question than a statement. His face says he wasn't expecting that answer.

He bends over, takes one foot out of his pants, and swings them off to the side. He grabs a coat off the rack behind him, folds it up, and puts it on the floor between his feet. He then lies back in the chair again, getting comfortable.

"Don't be afraid," he says with a warm smile. "Get on your knees and enjoy."

I kneel on the coat. I can smell a light, manly smell. The mix of cum from our earlier wank and a touch of sweat from the work day in his tight briefs. I wrap one hand around his cock at the base. It feels slightly slimmer than mine, but so much more shaft is left. I open my mouth wide. I put the head a few inches in without touching my mouth before I close my lips around it and let my tongue flick the bottom behind his head. Jon moans, "Yeeeeahhhhh. I haven't gotten head in a long time." My cock is uncomfortable straining against my briefs. I never adjusted it to the side before I got hard. Even though I came earlier, it's harder than I've ever felt it. I move my head slowly up and down a few times. Then, suckle it like a pacifier. This makes Jon moan louder. I taste his precum leaking out. "Oh yeah, baby. That's so good." I roll my eyes to look up. His head is tilted back, eyes closed. I'm sure he's imagining some co-ed, but I'm glad it's me getting a taste.

I never imagined the sensation of sucking a cock would be so wonderful or get me so horny. I start to explore more. I let go of his shaft and reached for his balls. So much skin and thick, coarse hair. I fondle his balls, never pausing my slow sucking while I play with them. I finally cup his balls, wrapping my finger and thumb around the top of the sack. I pull gently. "Yeah.

Tug my balls, just like that." I adjust to a better kneeling position to free up my left hand I was using for balance. I run it under his shirt. He's got just a bit of a belly above the waist, like maybe an inch that would poke out over his waistband. The fur on his belly is thick and luscious. I run my figures through it. I want to pull his shirt up, but don't want to overstep. I rub higher, pushing my luck, but never missing a lick sucking his cock. I finally reach his chest, and his hair feels even thicker and longer. My hand brushes a nipple. He inhales sharply while a big ooze of precum hits my tongue. I gently rub and flick his nip with my finger. It feels tiny but perky. He moans with every touch.

I've tried a few different moves with my mouth and tongue by this point, finding the techniques I like and, more importantly, the ones that make his cock jump or him moan. I continue the ones that get the biggest responses.

His moans get louder. He runs his hand through my hair. I look up again. This time, he's looking at me. "You're a natural cocksucker, aren't you, boy?" My cock strains against my pants. I'm sure I'm leaking up a storm. I nod a little and half blink, slowly, signaling, 'Thank you'.

I remember I noticed his strokes earlier that day. I take short ones, focusing just behind the head. He would alternate from that to full, long strokes on his shaft. He really seems to like it. I get braver. I move my left hand on his balls and my right to his spit-slick cock. I stroke with my head movements to work his whole shaft. My horniness has overridden any nerves. I start going deep, taking more in my mouth. He moans with every increase. I hold his cock at the base, hand flat against his pubes now. I get five inches in, then nearly six. Six, then six and a half, but I almost choke.

I pause and continue to work my tongue. I slowly move forward, going all the way until my nose is on his pubes. The downward curve slips past my uvula. I can't breathe, but it's exquisite. He lets out a low moan, more of a growl. I pull halfway out and slowly do it again. He runs his hand gently through the hair on the side of my head. I look up at him looking at me. "What a talent you have, son." Every time he calls me that, my cock gets impossibly harder. I want to please him. My lust makes me overestimate my abilities. I go all the way down again, too fast. I gag. I pull away from his cock, coughing. I try to catch my breath. His voice is still gentle but hornier. His expression on his face seems more randy. "Hmm. I kind of liked that."

I think of what he said to the magazine earlier, but dismiss it. I couldn't adjust my cock while kneeling, so I take the chance now to try and get it in a more comfortable position. He notices. "Oh, man," Jon says, "that must be uncomfortable. Just take your clothes off." I stand up, pull off my shirt, and kick off my shoes. "Look at that wet spot!" Jon exclaims. There's a spot 4 inches in diameter on my pants. My briefs are soaked. I shuck them off together.

Jon says, "So...you want to try to shoot a real second load in a day?" He's playful in his question, almost excited to help me pass a milestone.

"Sure," I say. My cock pointed out at him. A precum drool hanging off the end is about four to five inches. He reaches down to his briefcase, then fumbles to open a compartment atop it. He hands me a tube. "That's the good stuff. It's a little bit harder to clean up, but worth it."

As I take it out of his left hand, he takes his right forefinger and catches my precum drool without touching my cock. He sucks it off his finger. My eyes go wide. "Sweeter than mine," he says. "Not too much to start," nodding to the bottle I hold. I put a little in my hand. He grabs the bottle and adds some more. "About that much," Jon smiles, then sets the tube on his briefcase.

I smear it on my cock and start to stroke. It's so

slick. It's not better than what I normally do dry, but it's a wonderfully different sensation. I feel like I could last longer like this, and I can tell I won't chafe.

"Yeah, buddy. Stroke that beautiful cock. Enjoy your man meat." He says playfully but with a bit more grunt to his voice. "Come closer." He waves in with both hands. He leans forward, grabs my hips, and pulls me in as far as I can go. I inhale sharply as our thighs touch. He tucks his cock behind my balls. It's long enough to touch my taint, and the angle he's sitting at pushes it gently against the back of my sack. I dribble a blob of precum on his bush.

"Hmm," he says, "don't want to get my shirt dirty. He starts to unbutton it from the bottom. I stroke slower. The long strokes with the lube are better than I thought. He's watching my face, but I'm watching his torso, waiting to see his fur. He makes sure not to open it as he unbuttons. "You like men with hair, huh?" I nod, looking up to see him stroking his beard at me. He's teasing me. I look back down, agony in anticipation. I can see a slow, long dribble hanging from my cock. He pops his shirt open, tucking it behind him. He forces his belly to poke out and sits up just enough to catch this foot-long dribble glistening on top of his belly hair. I stroke faster, taking it all in. It's darker than his bush and less red than his beard. It's even thicker looking than it felt. His nips are tiny. Areola, too. And light pink like his cock head. He rubs his hands through his fur, showing it off for me. He pulls on his nipples. I feel his cock leak on the back of my sack as he does. "Yeah. You like all this fur." He rubs it some more. "You want to cum on my thick fur?" he asks. I nod. "Well, get down there and suck me off, then you can shoot your load on me while you still taste my cum."

I kneel again. I start sucking him harder, stroking faster than before. He grabs me by the back of the head. "Goddamn, you're a good little cocksucker." His voice is the guttural, lustful one from before, but more so. His eyes are closed, and his head tilted back again. I can tell he's gonna trash-talk like earlier today, but I have no idea what he's gonna say. He starts to thrust. "That's a good girl. Take daddy's cock." He really starts to face fuck me. He holds my head where I can't back off. I start to gag. "YEAH. Choke on my big cock, you dirty whore. Swallow every drop of my load." My mind is split, concentrating on breathing and realizing that I could cum with one graze of my cock. I use both hands against his thighs to just barely keep him from gagging me while I catch my breath through my nose.

I need to send him over the edge or risk passing out. I grab his sack and tug with my left hand while twisting a nip with my right. He growls like an animal. One thrust all the way, this time, it manages to go down my throat instead of stabbing me in the back. He begins to shoot. I can't believe the force of it coming out. I begin to naturally swallow to clear my throat. The motion of my throat and tongue is driving him wild. "Yeah. Swallow every drop. Oh, your throat is tighter than any pussy I've ever had." I've lost count, swallowing at least 10 or 12 spurts. "Don't stop. Don't stop."

I continue to swallow, feeling his head flare, still stuck in my throat just past my uvula. "I'm gonna come again!" He yells. "Ahhhh," he screams as three more big spurts shoot down my throat. He lets go of my head, collapsing in the chair. I pull his cock out enough to catch my breath. Sure, I'm purple in the face. I work my tongue gently, getting the last few drops from his second orgasm. I thought he'd passed out, but as soon as I took his cock out, he looked down at me.

"Come here. Quickly." He waves me to him with his hands again. I stand up. He closes his legs, still waving. I straddle him. He pulls me by the hips as he swings the arms of the chair out of the way. He pulls me down until I'm straddling his belly. His fur tickling my balls. His softening cock tickling my crack. He takes my hand

and spits in it to rewet the lube a bit. "Show me you can come twice today. Make me proud."

I start to stroke. I can taste his cum in my mouth. Thick and viscous. Slightly tangy, slightly salty.

"Yeah. Stroke it. Look at how much you're leaking on me." There's a puddle forming on his sternum. "There's nothing like cumming. Even better cumming with your buddies. No emotion. Just raw, animal lust. The need for release." I rub his chest fur with my free hand. I thrust, tickling my balls against his belly. "Yeah, that's it, buddy. Get that second load of cum out. It's gonna feel great." He reaches up and gently twists my nipples. Electricity flows from them to my cock. I moan and throw my head back. "Yeah," he says louder. "Cum for me, son."

That's all it takes.

I moan loudly, involuntarily. Jon gets louder. "Yeah, that's it. Cover me in spunk." I look down at him. He looks in my eyes. I've never felt so many spasms having an orgasm. They're still going.

"Shoot that jizz all over me, son."

"Yes, daddy," I say breathlessly.

"Yeah, son. Empty those balls!" Jon reaches down and cups my balls.

I instinctively stand a little, allowing him to wrap his finger and thumb around the top of my sack.

"Ooohhh!" I make the sound involuntarily again. "Pull 'em. Pull 'em." He gently tugs my sack. "Further," I say. He stretches my tight sack as much as he can.

"I'm gonna cum again, daddy."

"Hell yeah, son." He flat-palm slaps my chest. "Drain those balls."

I look down. He's already covered in more cum than I've ever made in my whole life. Just one big puddle below my cock. I quickly run my hand through it, getting as much as possible for additional lube.

"Fuck yeah, you dirty fucker." Jon says, "Jerk with that cum lube."

"I'm so close." I'm stroking faster than ever.

I watch him rub the index finger on his free hand in cum puddle, getting a big glob on the end. He reaches down, moving between my balls and thighs. He wipes the glob on my butthole. The sensation is intense.

"Uh. I'm gonna shoot," I say softly, still looking at him while he's looking where he's guiding his hand. He pushes the tip of his finger in my hole. Not even inside, just starting to spread the hole. It sent me over the edge. I breathe in deep.

He looks me in the eye. "Come, boy!" He commands. "Do what your daddy says, son." He wiggles his finger just a little. I growl this time. An uncontrollable animal noise I didn't know I could make. I shoot again. Just a few spurts, but still satisfying. My balls are like they've been turned inside out. Completely drained. He lets go of my sack. I guess his finger came out as I started cumming.

I waddle backwards. My hips hurt a bit from straddling. "See I told you you could cum more than once a day," he laughs back in his mild-mannered voice. He beams with pride. "Two in a row," he continues, "I'm impressed." I lean against the desk, spent. He grabs a couple of shirts from the laundry bag for us to each wipe off.

As we clean ourselves up, he says, "You're a natural. I don't know if you'll figure out if you're gay or bi, but I've never had a blow job that good before."

"Thanks?" I say awkwardly. Not embarrassed, just unsure.

He laughs.

"I hope I wasn't too rough. I kind of just let my cock take over and lost my manners," He says with a sheepish crooked smile.

"I mean...maybe a little. You know, for my first time," I say with a chuckle. "It caught me off guard, but I don't think I hated it."

He laughs as we start to get dressed.

As we walk out, I say, "I'm not opposed to doing that again...if you want."

Jon smiles, "Yeah. I wouldn't mind figuring out how to find a circle-jerk club again. I'm sure there's other guys, your age to mine, that don't get enough. We'd just have to find them and a place to meet. There's something primal about cheering each other on that's just a different kind of satisfying. I'd like to give a good pounding more often, but a jerk group would be better than by myself."

"Yeah," I say. "That could be a lot of fun." I pause. "I meant the other stuff, too."

"Oh." Jon shrugs. "Never say never. But I should be honest. I don't want to get your hopes up. These last few days have been the best male bonding I've had in years. But I'm not gay. The role-playing was good, but I approached it like a mentor. Helping you explore yourself and get past the next hurdle. Learning there's no limit to the heights of ecstasy you can achieve."

I'm a little bummed, but glad he let me know before I fantasized about anything further between us. "Thank you for your honesty. And thanks for being a," I make air quotes, "'big brother' about teaching me stuff." He tousles my hair. "That's what friends are for," he says with a smile. "You know what? We got busy, and I never got back around to talking about prostate massage. As Bate Bros now, I feel obligated to tell you about it." We both laugh. "Next time we're scheduled together."

I nod, and we both get in our cars.

# 4

## A FEW MONTHS

I have the next 2 days off. Wednesday, when I arrived after class, Jon finished his regular morning shift and put his things in his briefcase. A week ago, it would have been a quick hello. Maybe a courteous "what's new?" small talk conversation. I'm wondering if things will be awkward after last weekend's events. To my surprise, Jon gives me a big smile and a "Hey!" He shakes my hand and pats me on the shoulder. We have a brief chat like real friends with a longer history. He asks me about class. I asked about his weekend plans, which are mostly family-oriented. As he leaves, I feel good that it isn't awkward. And, while he wouldn't be a best friend, he'd be someone I could hang out with and have a good time.

ANOTHER CONVERSATION INVOLVES HIM LAMENTING about boredom and lack of joy in his life. I tell him how I found a group of people around the time I turned 18 that got me out of my shell. We have similar interests, like music and games. We have a regular game night. I talk about how I've learned it's important to have a social outlet, especially away from the pressure of dating (and sex, I think to myself). He nods and tells me he has been considering golf again. He quit after their first child was born. I encourage him to try that out.



ONE TIME, HE ASKS IF I'VE HAD ANY DATES LATELY. I tell him about a girl from class who made a move on me. We hooked up, and I lost my 'virginity' (in the typical sense) with her. He beams with pride. "She was a fast one? Made the moves. You lucky dog, you!" he says, punching my arm and tousling my hair. I smile, embarrassed. I don't tell him that while I enjoyed it, I was thinking about him and the guys from the magazines more than her. I did admit that, being my first time, I didn't last very long, and I think she wanted someone with more experience since I hadn't heard from her since. He comforts me with a single arm around my shoulder. I look up at him standing beside me. "That happens to a lot of us the first time, my friend," patting my shoulder. "You'll do much better next time. At least you've got the first one out of the way to help your nerves." I nod, truly thankful for the support, hoping he doesn't notice I'm half-hard from his arm around me.

DURING SOME OF THESE CONVERSATIONS, HE ALSO occasionally complains about his wife, and not just the lack of sex. I sometimes make a comment like, "At least you have your morning routine," or something like that. He'll chuckle, but it never spawns a conversation about any titillating topics. I've also noticed that if he is working to cover someone outside his normal weekday daytime shift, I haven't been on the schedule with him. It could be a coincidence since that doesn't happen often, so I try not to take offense. I am enjoying the camaraderie either way.

· · ·

IT'S BEEN MAYBE 3 MONTHS SINCE THAT WEEKEND. I come in on a Friday, and Jon's already packed his stuff to head home, but it seems he was waiting on something. I think maybe I'm reading too much into it. I get a big, happy "Hey!" from him and the arm around the shoulder again, which has only happened the one other time, which I felt was more consoling than this. He's more of a handshake guy. Plus, there's a few people in earshot, so I'm a little off guard. "I was hoping I'd see you before I left. I'm hoping you don't mind, but I've got you down to come in early Sunday. I'm covering again and want to get some inventory stuff worked on. You don't mind, do you?"

I reply, "Not at all." Knowing we open at noon on Sunday and he usually comes in before 11, I ask, "How early?"

He laughs. "9?" he says in a question that sounds more like "hope that's okay" than "feel free to counter."

"See you then," I reply, and he walks out the door.

# 5

# ANOTHER SUNDAY

J on is just getting out of his car as I pull in the lot at 9 a.m. Sunday. He waves and smiles enthusiastically, which gives me a warm feeling. I really enjoy how our friendship has grown, even if it is within the confines of the workplace.

We make our way into the back room of the store, and he tells me, "We're not really doing inventory." I look at him, confused. "I'm keeping my word. I promised to teach you about prostate massage."

I'm sure my face is showing mild shock. "Oh," I say. "Fun." I pause and look at my feet briefly as I scuff at a spot on the floor. "I thought you didn't want to do that kind of thing anymore."

He looks a little flush. He shrugs and kind of looks away, "Well." He turns back to look me in the eye. "Full disclosure. I value the bond we've created. To be completely truthful, I have been a bit hesitant. I'm not attracted TO you. Oh, that came out wrong. I'm not attracted to men in the way that I think you're looking for. And I didn't want to risk you getting attached. I'm also at odds about doing things behind my wife's back, even though she is a frigid bitch. If I'm going to cheat, I should be getting some poon." His manner is a bit more gruff. He takes a cleansing breath and more calmly says, "But then...I think about those circle jerks back in the day. And you and I have a real chemistry of some kind on top of being a great friend. You've been a good influence on me; you have gotten me to take up golf and other hobbies again. I've made some burgeoning friends through that. So when I saw I'd have to cover today anyway, I thought, 'What the hell?'" he shrugs as he says that. "I feel like we've had enough time for neither of us to run into emotional complications, and we can just have some good ol' bate bro fun."

I appreciate his honesty. I nod and say, "Sounds like a plan to me."

Now, he flushes and looks down while scuffing at the floor with one of his shoes. "Annnnnddd...I owe you the complete truth." He looks me in the eyes, "I haven't had my morning 'me' time since Monday, and that might have nudged my judgment when it occurred to me looking at the schedule."

I laugh. "At least you're honest about it."

He grabs a plastic grocery bag from his briefcase, and we walk over to the big table in the middle of the workroom again. He starts to unbutton his shirt, so I follow suit.

He begins," I get massages every few weeks. I started after a back injury a few years ago, but I found it beneficial, so I made it a regular routine. I used to just go for the cheapest and tried a bunch of different people. I would always pop a boner, so when I flipped over on my back, it was standing straight up under the sheet over me. Women would mostly avoid the area. Men would just kind of nudge it out of the way if needed with their arm."

We were already naked at this point. I was fully hard with a big droplet forming on my tip.

He says. "Eventually, one slightly older lady, probably my age now, asked if I wanted a happy ending. I said ok, not knowing what it was. In the last 15 minutes of the massage, she jerked me off. I slept like a baby that night. I went back to her again. 'You're back,' she said to me. I nodded, clarifying why I was back with the look on my face. About 15 minutes in, she whispered in my ear, 'Do you want your prostate massaged?' and I said, 'I guess.' She took some massage oil, rubbed it on my hole, and told me to relax, but to say something if it hurts. I'd had a prostate check during a complete physical once, so I kind of knew what to expect. But once she hit the spot and kept rubbing it, I covered her table in precum. She only did about 5 to 10 minutes, but boy was I primed. When she jerked me at the end, I popped quickly and more than I'd ever shot in my life."

I was breathless at this story. Aching to stroke my cock while he talked, but I wasn't sure if I would cum before we even started, so I didn't risk it.

He continues, "I brought the corn husker's lotion since it's what you have handy." I nod at his reasoning. "You can do it to yourself. When I'm really randy, I'll do it some. It isn't an easy angle, but it works. It's much better to have someone else do it." He pulls out some gloves, like at the doctor's office. "I'm pretty regular, if you catch my drift, so it shouldn't be too messy. But it is easier to clean up by throwing a glove away. They have them at the pharmacy. And some towels and baby wipes to clean up with." He goes down an aisle and gets a padded mat to lay on the table. I don't know where it came from. I'm impressed and humbled by how much effort he's put into teaching me about this.

"I'm going to let you do me first, and I'll talk you through it so you'll know what I'm doing when it's your turn. I think it'll help you relax more."

"Ok," I say with a little bit of nervousness in my voice.

He bends over the work table, resting his upper body on the table with his legs spread for balance, but no real weight on them. I've never seen his ass before. It's as hairy as his legs but looks twice as much where it combines in his crack. He pulls his cheeks apart. I can see his hole. "Take a good dollop of lube and rub it on the outside of my hole. Tease it. Help me to relax before you try to stick your finger in." I grab a glove and struggle to pull it on while he continues. "You'll likely want to use your index finger to start. To get lube in me for comfort. But you'll want to use your middle finger for the massage because it's longer."

"Gotcha," I reply as I open the lube. It's a full bottle, and a big glob plops out. I just kind of smear it on all sides of my thumb and first 2 fingers. I'm mesmerized by his furry ass and his light pink pucker. I rub lube gently on his hole, in a circle, like spiraling a drain in and out in the same direction. He moans. I drool precum on the floor. I can hear him taking deep, relaxing breaths. He's rock hard, it's pointing at the floor, but his pendulous balls cover most of it. I set the lube bottle down and cup his balls, lightly bouncing them. "Yeah," he moans softly. After a bit, he says, "Start to work it into the hole. Not too much at first. We're trying to lube it up gently."

I think about the tip of his finger he slid into me last time. My cock pulses at the thought. I push gently with the tip of my index finger. He moans as his hole pushes in, but doesn't open to let me pass. I wiggle my fingertip. He squirms. I decide he's not relaxed enough and go back to rubbing his hole. "Yeah, buddy. Gentle pressure like that. My hole will tell you when it's ready to open." I decide to give my finger a break. I let go of his balls and move to the side for a better angle. I transition without stopping, so the full pad of my thumb is rubbing, gently pushing his hole, and my other 2 fingers are pointing down, straddling his sack, my palm on his taint. His cock flexes hard as he sharply inhales. A large drop of precum falls to the floor from his cock. "Fuck, buddy!" breathlessly he says. "That feels incredible! What are you doing?"

"Hard to describe. I'll have to show you later."

"Well, keep it up."

After another minute of my rubbing and gently applying pressure to his hole, Jon says, "I think my hole is ready. Get that first knuckle in there."

Without returning to my index finger, I put a little more pressure, bending my thumb at the first knuckle. It gently slips right in.

"Oh Fuck. You're gonna have to show me that trick. I'm glad I can't touch my dick because I wouldn't be able to hold back."

I wiggle a little while and decide to switch fingers and go deeper. I pull out my thumb and line up my middle finger. It easily slides to the 2nd knuckle. He moans. "Go all the way," he almost whispers. As my 2nd knuckle enters his hole, the tip of my finger feels a hard, smooth object. I keep pushing, pressing slightly on the object. He moans, his legs shake, his cock drools a constant stream to the floor. I keep pushing until I can't get any further. I hold still, other than a little wiggling movement.

"Fuck yeah," He pants. "Did you feel it? Like a walnut?"

"Yes. That got a reaction out of you."

He chuckles. "Now just work that walnut gently. In, out, side to side. Experiment. You'll figure out what works best from how loud I get."

I chuckle this time, thinking, "I know that's right."

I do as he says. He writhes and moans. An occasional drip of precum adds to the puddle forming on the floor. I repeat the things that he responds to most. I've lost track of time. I'm in a trance looking at his hairy ass and balls dangling back and forth.

He snaps me out of it, saying, "You know some men can cum just from prostate stimulation. I need some direct cock attention to finish, unfortunately. The prostate isn't the only source of pleasure. If you remember from our last experiment, your hole alone can heighten your experience." He holds a hand up. His middle finger is on top of his index finger, making them almost the same length. "Try this on me," he says.

I do as he asks. It's tighter. I get to the first knuckle. He moans loudly. "Slowly," is all he says. I twist it a little. "Yeah," he whispers. He takes a deep breath. I gently push as he exhales. "Yeeeeahhhh." He says as I get past the second knuckle. I'm rubbing his walnut left and right as much as possible, as I can barely reach it. He pants in ecstasy. "Mmmm. I love you stretching my hole while you rub my button." I do another minute or so, and he says, "Are you ready to try?"

I pull my finger out. "Throw that glove away." He says as he's getting up off the table. He's standing by the time I turn back around. I take in his thick fur and long cock standing straight out except for the slight downward bend the last few inches. "Man, you enjoyed that. I don't think I've seen you that hard," he says. Mine usually stands straight out. This time it is so hard, it's pointing up almost 45 more degrees. "I can't wait to see how you react to this," He laughs, clapping me on the shoulder.


 my legs instead of holding any weight on them.

I jump as the cool lube touches my hole.

"My bad," he says. " I should have warned you."

"It's ok," I mumble with my head turned sideways, lying on the table.

"Do you want me to walk you through it?"

"No, I know what to expect now. I think you might be able to judge when my hole is ready better than I can."

"Well, say something if it's too much, or you need more lube."

I just nod.

He gets my hole wet, then quickly goes to teasing/probing it with his fingertip. I moan with every little push. "Yeah, buddy. Relax and enjoy." After a few minutes, he says, "Deep breaths in, then out."

On my second exhale, he gets into the first knuckle. "You ok?"

I take another deep breath in and out to relax. "It doesn't hurt, I just needed to adjust."

He pats the small of my back, "Good man."

He wiggles his fingertip. I squirm in delight.

"I want to get a little more lube in there. I'm going to the second knuckle."

I nod. It slips fairly easily, but he says, "Damn, you're tight." He hasn't gone too deep yet, but I feel lubed up enough to continue. "I'm switching to my middle finger...It's a little thicker."

As he pulls out. "Hey! What did you do to me earlier?"

I don't speak. I hold my hand up to show him. I make an inverted Y with my thumb sticking up. I wiggle my thumb to show how I was rubbing, and then I bend my first knuckle to show him how I slipped in.

"god-damn," he exaggerates the word.

I feel his thumb rub my hole. The full pad of it is less blunt than this fingertip. I moan. I still have my hand up, showing the position, paralyzed with pleasure. But I manage to flex my 2 fingers down. He sees out of the corner of his eye.

"Oh," he realizes. He pushes those 2 fingers down my taint, forcing my tight, drawn-up balls away from my body. His palm is warm on my taint. He rubs the hole faster in a circle, then rapidly jiggles left and right. Did I growl or squeal? I'm not sure. I can hear him mumbling affirmative words under his breath.

"Yeah. That's loosening you up," he says as he bends his thumb into my hole. I instinctively lift my legs off the table in pleasure. An actual volley of precum shoots out. He wiggles the first knuckle of his thumb around, relaxing my hole.

"Relax...relax." he rubs a small circle on my back to get me back in position. I relax my legs again.

"That hole was too tight before. This ought to go better."

He switches to his middle finger. As he slides in, he says, "It's still tight, but you're taking it."

He doesn't pause. He goes all the way in, pressing my prostate as he passes. I let out a low "Fuuuuckkkk."

"Look, Mikey, I think he likes it," he says with a dirty laugh.

He slowly pulls out, just clearing my prostate, and then back in. Applying pressure the whole way. "You like it when I work that magic button, huh?" His voice is rougher. I'm too zoned out in pleasure to pay attention to the fact that his animal instincts are taking over again.

Over the next few minutes, he moves from stimulating my prostate to almost finger fucking me.

The lube is drying out. I manage to say, "It's starting to hurt." He sounds like he was zoned out, and I snapped him out of it. "Huh? Oh. Sorry about that, buddy. Glad you said something." His voice softens by the time he finishes talking.

He pours a little more lube from the bottle, and it feels good again. He rubs my button for minutes; I have no sense of time. He pulls his finger out. I feel a different pressure on my hole. It's stretching further. "How's that?"

"Ok, so far." Almost a lie.

"It's so tight I can't even get the tip of 2 fingers in there. I wanted you to feel the stretch a bit. Try some deep breaths."

I concentrate on letting my body go limp while I breathe.

After about a minute, he pulls out the two fingers that aren't even in to the first knuckle and says, "I'll try something else. I want you to sample all the pleasures. But you may just be too tight."

I feel a broader pressure on my hole. I assume he's

using his thumb again. It feels great. It's not going in, but the pressure is pleasant.

"Just breathe deep. On the relaxing exhale, you push back. You're in control." His voice is calming.

With every breath, I push back a little further. Pleasure in the pressure. He rubs my back in a circle again. I relax further. I push back again, and "pop," it slips inside. I gasp. It's on the cusp of pain. I understand what he meant about the pleasure in stretching the hole.

"Oh, wow," I gasp. "That's intense."

"You should see the stream of precum you're making," he says.

"Fuuuuuck. Is that 2 fingers or 2 thumbs?" I ask. "The stretch feels almost too much."

He says softly, in a lusty voice, "It's my cock head."

I moan at the thought.

"You want a little more?"

I swallow hard, my mouth dry. I can only nod.

He slowly pushes further. My legs shake as his downward-curved cock presses intently on my prostate. He can tell when he's past it as I stop gasping in air. He slowly moves back, my legs shaky. I'm glad the table is supporting my weight.

He does a few slow strokes in and out, really working my button with the head of his cock.

He stops rubbing my back. He grabs my hips with both hands and continues his slow pumps.

"Fuck. This is incredible," he says in a raspy, almost growl. "I heard it was good, but I never imagined."

He pulls my hips with his thrusts. He's making more grunting noises.

"This is the best pussy I've ever fucked. I could ride this sweet, tight hole all night."

I'm succumbing to the intense pleasures, but my subconscious knows that voice belongs to the man that gagged me skull fucking me. I ignore it and focus on my prostate getting pummeled and the stream of precum I can feel flowing through my cock.

He's getting faster and deeper. I can feel he's hitting a wall, the top of my rectum. My hole begins to hurt. I lift up my head and turn it slightly. "I need more lube," I mutter.

He grabs me by the neck with one hand and shoves me back down. He pulls halfway out, spits a big loogie on his shaft, and shoves it back in. I wail with the first shove, but it works. My hole is slick enough to handle the assault he's dishing out. He continues to fuck me harder, panting with every stroke. I can feel his sweat falling on me. He's mumbling again. Things like, "Yeah. You like that big dick, don't you?" I know he's not talking to me in his mind, but I'm writhing in pleasure and don't care. He's still hitting the wall inside me.

"Why can't I get these last two inches in?" He's taking long thrusts now. My hole and prostate are taking a beating with every stroke.

My balls begin to tighten. "I'm gonna cum." I whisper. He doesn't notice. Uncontrollably, I say it louder, "Oooooh, I'm gonna cum.

He lets go of my neck and grabs both hips again. He switches to longer strokes.

Panting between each sentence, Jon says in a rough voice, consumed by wild abandon, "You gonna cum? You gonna cum without touching your dick? Is my big cock gonna make you cum, you little faggot? You like my cock buried in you, you dirty fucking whore? You like me plowing your tight little faggot pussy?"

I say "Yes" after each question. Louder each time. He continues to thrust, but slower. Pulling all the way out and popping his head through my hole with each thrust, and not stopping until he hits the wall inside. On the 3rd stroke like this, I yell louder than I ever have as I begin to cum hands-free.

"Oh fuck yeah!" he yells as my ass starts to clench down on his shaft with each spasm I have. He's as far in as he can go. He makes short movements staying as far in as he can, letting my quaking hole massage his cock.

"Oh, god. I've never felt anything like this," he screams.

I've lost count of the number of spasms I've had. More than I thought I was capable of. More than when I got to cum in his fur.

"Don't stop! Don't stop!" I don't know who's saying the words. I realize it's me. "Don't stop," this time voluntarily adding, "I'm gonna cum again."

"Fuck yeah," Jon pants in a growl. He continues his perfect strokes.

As my orgasm starts again and my hole tightens around his shaft, Jon yells, "Aaaahhhh! Fuck! I'm cumming. I'm cumming." He stops thrusting. Letting my contractions massage him into orgasm.

I feel the explosion adding to my already half-full rectum. The cum starts to shoot out of my hole around his cock. Neither of us has as many waves as the first orgasm, but it seems close to Jon's normal number of spasms for both of us.

Jon growls as he pulls out. I'm too weak in the legs to move. I can see peripherally that he's pacing a bit. He's still in his animal mode, but more so this time. His face looks closer to testosterone rage than post-sex glow. Grunting and panting. He throws his head back, closes his eyes, and takes deep breaths. He calms as he continues to breathe. As his breathing slows, he tilts his head forward, eyes still closed. His face is relaxed, closer to the way mine feels. I'm looking over my shoulder at him, still lying on my stomach. He opens his eyes. He looks me in the eyes. He smiles and has the afterglow of pleasure. His eyes move down my body, looking at the scene.

His face changes to panic. He covers his mouth. "What have I done?" repeating over and over again.

He gets the baby wipes and bends to clean me up, but stops short. His eyes wide, he asks, "Are you ok? Did I hurt you? Your poor hole."

I reach back. I can feel it's stretched, gaping open,

not quite the width of his shaft. He gently wipes my crack. He looks at the wipe. I can tell he's checking for blood. There isn't any I can see. He's mumbling, almost whimpering, "I can't believe I lost control. I'm so sorry. I shouldn't have done that. Forgive me." I'm not sure if he's talking to me or himself. I'm too exhausted to care.

He goes through several wipes, cleaning my crack, taint, balls, and shaft. I finally say, "Can you help me up? This isn't comfortable to lie here this long."

He gasps, "Oh my god, I'm so sorry. I should have realized your legs might not work." he gently helps me up. I chuckle as I see the puddle of precum and jizz on the floor. It's over a foot in diameter.

"Bit of a mess," he says, attempting to hide his quivering voice. It finally occurs to me he's Jekyll and Hyde. I kind of feel bad for him. A hidden side of desires he can't reach. Probably not gay ones like I'd like him to have. Just raw, aggressive sexual energy. Yet here he is, back to the mild-mannered sweetheart everyone sees daily. "Here. Sit on the table." He helps me up on the mat that covers the table. I lie back and rest while he cleans the floor. I doze off. I wake to find him tenderly cleaning more cum off of my thighs and crotch. I smile at him. He tries to return it. Weakly, he starts," I'm so very sorry. I completely lost control. I called you horrible names. I'm ashamed I used those words...and I used you in such an awful way. I can't ever make that right."

I cut him off, "It may not be the experience I would have chosen, but...at least I wasn't scared because it was you. Give yourself a little credit. You did get me relaxed and prepared." He looks away but nods.

I say, "Now help me up off this table."

He does. He goes to throw away the baby wipes in his hand. I reach behind me and feel my hole. As he comes back around the corner, I bend over and pull my cheeks apart, "See. It's almost back to normal."

He tries to manage a smirk, but I can see he's still bothered by what happened. Was it the taking advantage of me and having his way? Is he questioning his sexuality? Is it solely because I'm a man? My mind spirals with wonder in the haze of such a heavy post-sex euphoria.


After we're dressed, he tells me I should go home and rest. I protest, but he insists. I relent, mainly because my hole is quite sore. I ask, "How will you handle the store alone?". He says, "I'll let the returns pile up. I can tell the others you got sick."


I don't see him for a few weeks. He leaves early from his regular shift. He's finally there one day when I come in. I smile, glad to see him. I've missed our talks. He smiles, but it's not the gleam it was before. He says softly, "What I did was wrong, but avoiding you the last few weeks was wrong, too. You've been a friend, giving me good advice. I should have been here if you needed me."

"It hurt my feelings a little. I really did miss the friendship and conversations from the last few months," I confess to him. "But I also wasn't completely surprised."

He nods. His face is hiding strong emotions I can't quite decode.

"So, how's your golf game progressing?" I ask to lighten the mood.

He lights up a little and tells me about last weekend's amazing game.

We chat most weekdays in passing after that, but he never does schedule us alone again.

# EPILOGUE

I eventually went off to a four-year college. I came home for the summer and stopped by the shop on a weekday morning to see if they needed any help so I could earn a little cash while I was home. Jon had a huge smile as I walked around the corner. He stood and gave me a full-on bear hug.

"I've missed you. And our chats."

"Me too," I say.

I ask about working over the summer.

"Sure, we can use your help. Not as many of our prom season workers stayed on this year."

In a low voice, "I have so much news to tell you. All good. Most of it is thanks to you."

I laugh, then catch myself to quiet the volume. "That's great." I pat his shoulder this time. I'm proud of him.

"Can I take you to lunch?" he asks.


"...AND THEN, DURING THE DIVORCE, I GOT INTO therapy. I understand myself better now, not just sexually but overall. But also sexually, too," he says, a little excited. We both chuckle. "I've been reading up on what are apparently some of my kinks. And I'm developing better control at the moment. Not that I've had

99

much chance to practice it." He pulls a face with a shrug on that last comment.

"That's great. I'm really proud of you. You'll find some kinky broad one of these to give you a run for your money," I poke fun at him. He laughs. I shake my head. "Your own apartment/bachelor pad. Haha. I bet it's covered in spunk."

He beams, "My record is five times in one day."

We both laugh.

"Now I can have porn, lube...I got 3 different kinds of varying slickness. Oh, and a fancy prostate thing that looks like aliens made it but man, does it add to the experience."

I just smile and shake my head.

"What about you?" he asks. "Dating anyone?"

"Not dating, no."

"Oh?" he raises his eyebrows with the question.

"I've managed to have a little fun."

"Ladies?" Still curious about my sexuality, I think.

"One. After a drunken frat party. You would have been proud. I lasted much longer. She even finished first and second."

"That's my boy." He slaps the table. "But just one?"

"Welllllll...I found the campus glory hole in the upstairs library bathroom."

His jaw drops.

"I really like getting my dick sucked. Plus, I've gotten pretty good at sucking dicks."

Jon turns red, "You were already pretty damn good from what I remember."

I laugh.

"So, uh...the real reason I asked you here," he lowers his voice. "Between the locker room at my gym, the one at the golf clubhouse, and some heavy drinking with other frustrated married men, I've found a few guys interested in a circle-jerk club. I'm calling it The Brotherhood of Baters."

I chuckle, "Good for you. How have your 'meetings' gone?"

"Well, our first one is this weekend. And...I wanted to know if you'd like to join?" I give him a quizzical look. "You could be like my second in command." I can see the thrill on his face.

"Sure," I say. "Sounds great. Tell me more."

"I'm laying some ground rules with the guys. Male bonding and support are key, but cock gratification and exploration are equally important. Oh, let me tell you about the guys..."

# JOKER'S WILD
## BY PETER SCHUTES

# DOWNTOWN

Bo stood on the corner of Main and Fremont Street, mouth agape. He'd just stepped off the bus from Little Rock with little more than the clothes on his back and a dozen crisp twenties he stole from his alcoholic father. He didn't know what he wanted to do in the city built from sin, but he knew he'd taken his last beating from the wretch who'd raised him.

Bo was tall, with dusky brown skin the color of instant cocoa. His hair hung in loose curls. His t-shirt was tight and his jeans were loose. He'd learned to avoid tight jeans so as to conceal his disturbingly large cock. He could barely have a conversation if his jeans were tight enough to show a bulge. Guys and girls alike would just keep drifting off as their gaze returned to his crotch. Their eyes would glaze over with a mixture of fear, admiration, and lust. He imagined his face bore the same look of amazement right now, staring at the Glitter Gulch.

The heat was unbearable. As he walked past the Golden Gate, gusts of air conditioning blew from the front doors, beckoning gamblers in to escape the heat. What had caught Bo's eye, though, was the giant neon cowboy perched above the Pioneer Club. He'd left the oppression of the Arkansas hills to come to this wild, flat expanse. The smiling cowboy, with his red kerchief and cigar, embodied the freedom of the West.

It had only been five minutes since Bo stepped off the air-conditioned bus. The dry heat was refreshing, but it caused the armpits of his t-shirt to dampen and darken with perspiration. He ducked into the Pioneer Club just to cool off, hoping he'd see a real cowboy inside. Sadly, the clientele was nothing like the smiling, happy-go-lucky ranch hand that had beckoned him inside. At the nearest slot machine, an old man in a weather-beaten grey suit dangled a burning cigarette from his lips; a length of ash dropped into his can of coins. He didn't notice, transfixed, pulling on the one-armed bandit and muttering, "Come on. Just one more."

The carpet gave off a sour odor of beer, sweat, and cigarette smoke. A scantily-clad woman with long black cocktail gloves and a feather headdress approached him.

"Welcome. Can I get you some chips or maybe just some change to play the slots?"

Bo considered his limited fortune. He didn't know how to play cards or craps. He didn't like the odds at the roulette table. The slot machines looked like a long shot at best, but he needed to gamble if he wanted the goddess of good fortune to shine on him.

"I'll take some quarters." He gave her a twenty, and she produced two heavy rolls of quarters wrapped in brown paper.

"Good luck now, honey."

Bo decided that he wouldn't touch what came out of the slots. Whatever fortune had in store, he knew better than to gamble away whatever it gave, even if it was less than he'd started with. The machine he'd chosen was a tight slot. He went through an entire roll of quarters and had only produced 50 cents. He hesitated, wondering if he should waste another ten dollars.

"Fuck it." He tore open the roll and fed the machine quarter after quarter. His till had $1.25 when he reached his last quarter. He couldn't believe he'd almost lost his fortune. He put the last quarter in, pulled the arm, and watched as one, two, three bars lined up. A bell rang. Quarter after quarter spat out of the machine until his till was nearly full.

The change lady came over. "Lucky boy! What's say we trade those up for some silver dollars?"

Bo shook his head. "I'm ready to cash out."

The woman frowned. "You don't want to turn your back on Lady Luck now, do you?"

Bo smiled. "Yeah, I think I'd better."

All told, he'd won $501.25, a tidy sum. The wad of twenties in his pants had a few Franklins to keep them company. The urge to keep trying his luck was powerful, but Bo had integrity and willpower to keep him strong. He'd come to Las Vegas to work, not to gamble. It was time to find a room for the night and enjoy a good steak. He left the Pioneer Club feeling great.

That's when he saw him. A grinning cowboy with a red kerchief, a ten-gallon hat, a yellow pearl snap shirt, jeans, and a pair of Justins. He looked just like the neon cowboy. The handsome man turned and smiled at Bo.

"Welcome to the Pioneer Club, Pardner. Free drink?"

The cowboy handed Bo a poker chip with the words "Pioneer Club Casino" on one side and "One Free Drink" on the reverse.

Bo couldn't believe how stupid he'd been. A real cowboy in Vegas? Maybe ten miles out of town, but not on Fremont Street.

"You had me fooled there, for a second."

The cowboy grinned at Bo, an odd twinkle in his eyes. "You think I ain't a real cowboy? Think I don't know how to ride a horse?"

Bo got a queer vibe off the way the cowboy stressed the word 'horse.' Bo wasn't queer by choice, just by circumstance. He'd met a few women who wanted to try him, but they all backed away when he took it out and got hard. Men were different. They mostly gave up and ended up fucking Bo instead, but a few were brave enough to let him do the deed. He wondered if this cowboy could be in that club of men who shunned the company of women in favor of a more virile companion.

Bo knew the signals. He feigned absentmindedness as he adjusted his crotch. "What kind of horse you ride, then?"

The cowboy signaled back. He put his hand in the right rear pocket of his jeans and scratched his ass. "Depends on the size of the horse, don't it?"

Bo said, "I ain't got a room yet. You know any good ones?"

The cowboy said, "You can stay at mine. I'm off in an hour."

Bo said, "I'm looking forward to it."

To kill time, Bo went to the Golden Gate, where they sold a steak dinner for 50 cents. It was a loss leader to lure in gamblers, of course, but Bo was done gambling. He had a bird in hand now and didn't need to go bushwhacking. The steak was so big, it hung over the edges of the plate. Luckily, Bo was hungrier than a horse.

That cowboy was hot. He was maybe five years older than Bo, with a deep tan and gleaming white teeth. That back pocket ass scratch meant the cowboy wanted dick. Bo hoped he was ready for a Vegas-sized helping of his steak. If not, Bo didn't mind the backup plan. He'd learned to like the feeling of a hot cock unloading in his ass. It was relaxing, unless the guy was hung big. That was a turn-on, but it also meant hard work. Bo had enough dick to go around. He didn't need a big one. He liked the good-looking guys, no matter what was between their legs. As long as they could fuck him or take him, he was happy.

At midnight, Bo met the cowboy in front of the Pioneer Club. They nodded. The cowboy put an arm around Bo's shoulders and steered him off the strip.

"I got a place on Third Street. Follow me."

"Can I know your name, at least? I'm Bo."

The cowboy grinned, "Name's Grayson."

Two blocks off Fremont sat the Liberty Bell, a shabby bachelor's hotel with a neglected cactus in the entryway. The lobby hosted two dusty slots and a cigarette machine. Grayson the Cowboy popped in a quarter and got a pack of Lucky Strikes.

He said, "They cost fifty cents on the strip now. Can you believe those bastards?"

The rickety elevator brought them to the fourth floor. Down the hallway, Bo noticed a shared shower and toilet. Grayson's room was adjacent to the neon Liberty Bell sign, which illuminated it with a bluish hue, bright enough that no lights were needed.

Bo was conscious of his sweaty clothes. "Should I shower?"

Grayson put his hands under Bo's t-shirt and sniffed his armpits. "No. After." And he lifted the shirt up over Bo's head, exposing his muscular torso.

Grayson unsnapped his shirt in a rough tug with one hand while the other explored the contours of Bo's tight body. Bo felt a familiar warmth building in his crotch. He unbuttoned his jeans and let them fall to the floor. His boxers weren't long enough to cover his entire length. He shucked them, standing naked.

Grayson stepped back. It was Bo's favorite moment during the sex act, when the look of shock gave way to something else, something unpredictable.

Grayson's breath grew shallow as his eyes widened. "Good lord. Oh, man!"

There was that look of shock. Which deadly sin would come next? Fear? Envy? Lust?

It was lust. Grayson kicked off his boots, then

peeled off his jeans, revealing a modest cock and firm, round ass. He knelt on the floor. With both hands, he lifted the head to his mouth. Despite the extreme length and girth of his cock, the head was much smaller. It was a torpedo dick. Grayson was able to get the head and the first few inches into his mouth.

Bo leaned against the wall, letting Grayson's tongue bring him to full attention. Because Bo's cock was already so big, it didn't look like it grew much when it hardened. But there was a difference, and Grayson's jaws were all too aware of it. Soft, it fit nicely; hard, it was too much. Grayson did his best, but the thick cock was too hard and too big around to allow him access. Bo was familiar with this plight. He'd been left hanging more than a few times by guys who refused to do any sort of butt stuff and didn't want Bo to suck them off. Those were disappointments on his rejection list. He hoped Grayson wouldn't join them.

Despite being older than Bo, Grayson was still smooth and boyish. The cowboy spread out on the bed, his pretty penis throbbing invitingly. "Your turn."

Bo knelt and took the perfect pink package in his mouth. It was just long enough to tickle the back of his throat. He closed his eyes and lost himself in the act of oral service. His soft slurps and Grayson's shuddering breaths were the only sounds in the room. Outside, there were whoops, hollers, car horns, and buzzing neon signs. In Grayson's pad, there was only lovemaking.

Grayson used a foot to push Bo off of him briefly. He rolled back, exposing his twitching pink hole. Bo held Grayson's waist as he buried his tongue in the boy's ass. The cheeks were dusted with downy soft blond fuzz. It was like eating a peach. Every so often, Bo lifted his nose out of the butt crack to take a slurp of the Grayson's balls. Each time he did, the little cowboy wriggled as though it tickled.

Soon, the pink hole was sloppy with spit. Mix a

little grease with it, and it was ready to fuck. Bo hoped his cowboy was serious about riding horses. Bo's was the bucking bronco of cocks. Every ride was hard, fast, and left the rider sore. Was Grayson up to the challenge?

A tin of Albolene appeared as if out of nowhere. Buck greased up his cock and spat in his hand to add more viscosity. Grayson easily slid two greasy fingers in his hole. Bo's tongue work had clearly loosened him up.

Bo steeled himself for rejection as he pressed the small head of his cock inside the cowboy. An inch more, and the guy would either scream his head off or let him in. It was like a pull of the one-armed bandit. The odds weren't great. The few times Bo had gotten inside, it was great. He knew he couldn't go all the way, and satisfied himself with stroking the top of his cock against another man's hole. It was enough. One man had taken him as far as he could go, all the way to the back. He was nearly halfway inside him that time. It was a memory he clung to every time he got to this point with a man.

Grayson clenched his teeth, closing his eyes tightly.

"Should I stop?"

"Fuck no! Keep going!" To emphasize this, Grayson bent at the waist and grabbed one of Bo's butt cheeks, pulling him closer. Bo marveled as his girthy cock slipped further inside the thrashing cowboy. Then he felt it. The place he'd only felt once before. He was inside as far as he could go.

Bo began rocking his hips, moving in and out slowly, savoring the pressure against the shaft of his cock. The pleasure flowed down his shaft, warming his groin, causing his big dangling balls to churn. He felt them lift, first left, then right, until they were close to his body. Then the cycle started over, his balls dropping and lifting in a rhythm unrelated to his thrusts.

Grayson wrapped his arms around Bo's neck and whispered in his ear. "Deeper."

Bo shrugged. "Sorry, that's as far as it goes." He returned to the rhythmic humping that would soon lead to a satisfying orgasm.

Grayson hissed. "No. All the way." He hooked his ankles behind Bo's ass and pressed. As he did so, he twisted his body to one side. Bo felt something new. Something impossible. He was entering another hole. His small head felt a curtain of flesh give way, admitting him into a private back room that he'd never discovered in his twenty years of life. Grayson continued to squeeze Bo forward like a wrestler in a headlock. The curtain gave way, and with a rush, Bo's entire cock slid inside. For the first time, he felt his hips slam against another man's ass. He was all the way in.

Grayson thrashed and squealed, balling up fistfuls of sheets in his fingers. "Yes! Fuck me!"

Bo tested the depths, withdrawing until his head popped out of the inner hole, then pushing back in with some effort. Each time he did this, it got easier.

Grayson's glassy eyes fixed on Bo's. "Don't hold back, man. Fuck me hard."

Bo realized his entire sexual experience had been about holding back. In this moment at the Liberty Bell Hotel, in the blue-white light neon glow, he let go. He took massive strokes, long enough to fell a tree. It was freedom and pleasure he'd never thought could be his. Normal men knew something like it, but they could never know the satisfaction of the enormous strokes Bo made inside his cowboy. They would know only a fraction of the pleasure, for every inch of Bo's cock radiated a tingling glow that traveled from the tip to the base, up his spine, and into his brain. And there were so very many inches.

Bo's dusky skin beaded up with sweat. The droplets fell from his forehead and chest, adding to the beads of sweat already gathered on Grayson's face. The cowboy licked his smiling lips, eyes fluttering. He wrapped his arms around Bo's middle, giving him traction to push back as Bo pushed forward. They'd meet in the middle in an explosive thrust, then pull away in a long, long stroke. During one of the long outstrokes, Bo pulled out completely. He saw Grayson's hole gaping like a landed trout on the dock at Bull Shoals Lake. It clamped shut, then opened again as Bo forced his way back inside and down the long chute.

Grayson squirmed, holding his hard cock in his fingers, stroking softly. "Oh, fuck, I'm gonna come." And he did. A lot. His belly, chest, and chin were slick with it. As Bo continued to pound him, Grayson's cock grew soft and lolled gently from side to side as it shrank to the size of a peanut.

Bo loved seeing the little pink penis lying there helpless as his own monstrous dick heaved in and out of his prey. He felt proud, confident, powerful, and dominant. He'd fucked the cowboy into submission. He was in charge.

A few minutes later, Grayson's little dick was stiff again, throbbing hard against Bo's belly. It left a sticky, clear snail trail in Bo's pubes as it dribbled with anticipation of a second orgasm.

Grayson released one arm from around Bo's waist. He cupped Bo's large pectoral muscle in his palm and pinched the nipple. Bo was wired that way. It sent him across the precipice after which there was no retreat. It was that time.

Grayson murmured, "D'you like that?"

Bo nodded, pounding furiously. He felt the grip grow tighter until soon there was a mixture of pain and pleasure adding to his already growing orgasm.

"Fuck, I'm gonna come," said Bo.

"Oh, oh! Me too!" This time, Grayson came without touching himself. He thrashed from side to side, churning out more come than the last time. When Bo saw it, that was all he had left between him and orgasm.

"Yes!" He shouted loud enough to shake the dishes in the sink. His balls clenched tightly against his shaft as he felt the first warm tide grow hot. His cock let loose giant burps of semen inside Grayson. The burps became violent spurts as he hit his orgasmic stride. He held himself deep, pushing against the cowboy's butt, until he felt the last drops leave him. He squeezed his piss muscle, and a few more drops leaked out.

## COLD BACON

Bo didn't remember falling asleep; it happened so fast. The long bus ride with no sleep had finally taken its toll. When he awoke in the morning, his hardening cock was still firmly wedged inside Grayson. They went a second round, finishing quickly.

While Grayson cooked bacon on the hot plate, Bo wrapped a towel around his waist and headed to the hall shower. It was little more than two facing rows of shower heads. There were no bars of soap, only Borax dispensers. The powdery soap burned a little on his skin as he washed off the sex and sweat. He shut his eyes tightly and rubbed the abrasive cleanser on his face. He carefully rinsed, being sure to get any stray bits of the stuff out of the crevices near his eyes.

When he was satisfied that his face was squeaky clean, he put some in his hair, turned around, and leaned back. The sound of an astonished gasp opened his eyes.

Across from Bo was a thin, wiry kid about his age. Horror filled the kid's face as he stared mercilessly at the monster dangling there. Bo studied the boy's face as it melted from horror to amazement, then desire. Bo held his shaft at the midpoint, lifting the soft, growing flesh skyward. The kid needed no further signaling. In an instant, he was on his knees, gobbling the flesh in greedy gulps.

Bo was still soft enough that the kid got pretty far down the shaft. He was a talented cocksucker, for sure. Bo had rarely been that deep in a man's throat. But he was getting hard. The kid would give up, back away, return to his shower, or skulk off shamefully to his room. Bo started counting in his head, betting if it was less than twenty or more than twenty before this happened.

But it didn't happen. This kid was one in a million. He let Bo's huge cock inflate in his throat, holding his breath, giving his esophagus time to adjust. After a thirty-count, the kid pulled back, exhaling in a loud woof. But instead of giving up, he went back for more. Inch after inch of Bo disappeared down the kid's throat. He saw the outline as it pressed against the larynx. Again, the kid backed up, exhaled loudly, and went right back down for more. They were the only two men in there, but that could change in a moment. Bo worried about getting caught briefly. Then the boy's talented mouth convinced him to throw caution to the wind. He let the warm water cascade over his wide frame as he submitted to the cocksucker's talents.

As Bo had feared, another resident walked in on them. He had little to fear.

The newcomer, a handsome man in his forties with a furry chest and bulging biceps, laughed. "Randy, you giving the new guest the grand tour? When you're done, come over here and take care of this." He hung his towel on a hook and pointed to his impressive man-cock, half hard, surrounded by a thick black bush of pubic hair.

Randy just kept sucking Bo's cock while the newcomer lathered up using his own soap. The handsome older man let out a yelp when Randy pulled back with a cough of phlegm, exposing much of Bo's cock to his stare.

"Shit, that's a big dick. I thought I was big." In

truth, the man was very big, but he paled in comparison to Bo. "Fuck, Randy, he's gonna ruin ya."

Randy was in that place cocksuckers go to, where the outside world holds no meaning. He hummed and gulped, making greedy sounds, coughing and spluttering when he came up for air, returning to the blow job with enthusiasm after each long inhale. It was the way oral sex worked best. It's not about going deep or even going fast. It's about keeping a steady rhythm. Nothing makes a man lose a boner faster than a guy who stops to take a break. It's called a blow JOB for a reason. It's hard work. And Randy was a champion.

Bo felt the tingle of release. Some small bit of pre-ejaculate must have leaked out. Every talented cock-sucker knows this signal. They taste it, and it's time to cup the balls, work the shaft with one hand, and for god's sake, don't lose the rhythm. Randy knew all of this.

"Oh fuck, kid, I'm gonna come."

Randy kept at it silently, but Bo figured he was thinking, "No shit."

In great waves, the orgasm washed over Bo. Randy gulped and swallowed, unable to keep up with the flood that sprayed from the corners of his mouth. Vegas was a city of firsts. Last night, it was the first time he'd gone all the way inside a man. This morning, it was his first time coming down another man's throat. He had a feeling there would be more firsts to come.

Randy moved on. He cleaned the tip of Bo's dick, then moved on to the older man whose cock had blown up to a very impressive size.

Randy spoke for the first time. "Hey, Grant." It came out hoarse.

"Shut up and suck my dick."

Randy obeyed.

Bo toweled off and returned to Grayson's room, where the bacon was getting cold.

## ❧ 3 ❧

# CONFIRMED BACHELORS

A room at the Liberty Bell was twenty bucks a week, payable in advance. Thanks to Lady Luck, Bo was flush with cash, so he took a discount and paid $75.00 for a whole month.

The front desk clerk took the cash, fished for a key, and said, "Fourth floor, right?" He gave a meaningful wink.

Bo didn't quite get it. "Sure, I mean whatever floor has a room."

The clerk smiled coyly. "Oh, I think you want the fourth floor. It's where all the confirmed bachelors like to stay. You are a confirmed bachelor, yes?"

Bo wasn't a city slicker. He'd grown up thirty miles from Little Rock in a little hick town. But he wasn't dumb. He was able to put together what the clerk was saying. He'd heard a few names for it. This was just a new one.

"Yeah, I'm a confirmed bachelor."

When the clerk gave Bo the key, he took his hand and held it by the thumb. "My name's Carl. If you need any pointers about life in Sin City, be sure to ask. I'm a fountain of knowledge."

Bo smiled. "You know where I can get some work?"

Carl looked at Bo appraisingly. "Judging by what I see under that tight shirt, you're strong and well-put-together. They're building casinos on the Strip and need construction workers, if you have any talents in that area."

Bo sighed. "It's too damned hot. I'd rather work inside."

Carl nodded thoughtfully. "You look like someone who heats up easily. Maybe card dealing if you play cards?"

Bo shook his head. "I'd probably need some lessons."

Carl smiled. "Are you familiar with the oldest profession? That one's a lot of indoor work, and it pays well."

Bo scratched his head. The oldest profession? What did this guy mean?

Carl was not an unkind person. He genuinely wanted to help Bo. In a conspiratorial whisper, he said, "Prostitution."

Bo recoiled, stunned. "I'm a man. Women pay for it, too?"

The clerk gave a titter. "Well, yes, some. But mostly men. Eight million people come to Las Vegas every year. Six million of them are men, and a large percentage of them want to pay for sex. A small percentage of those men want...you know, a bachelor to keep them company. Someone tall, dark, and handsome."

Bo said, "I came to Vegas for a job. That ain't a job, is it?"

Carl said, "It pays handsomely. You can make ten or twelve bucks a day dealing blackjack, or two hundred bucks a night selling whatever you've got under those jeans. I can help you find either kind of work."

Bo said, "Uh, wow. Just wow. Maybe. How's it work?"

Carl whispered again. "Maybe you can show me what you're working with. There's different types."

Bo gave Carl an appraising look of his own. The guy was harmless. He bleached his hair and maybe wore a little eye makeup. Bo didn't care if the guy wanted a look. He didn't seem like the murdering type.

Bo said, "I'll give you a peek." He unzipped his jeans and pulled out his dick, letting it flop between his legs.

The clerk gave a startled gasp. "Gracious! That's a big one. You've got a gift, Bo. A real gift. Put that away, and I'll make some calls.

## ❈ 4 ❈
# RED TAIL

Bo had no illusions that the sex business was going to be on the up and up. He felt pretty sure that no matter what magic Carl tried to conjure, Bo would still end up in a miserable situation. He was only half right.

It was a lucky thing that Bo loved his big cock almost as much as he loved sex itself. That combination of confidence and craving are the perfect ingredients for a hustler to make his living. Lack of confidence gave off a stench that repelled clients. A disgust for the sexual act would make even the horniest trick lose his hardon. The men were paying to feel wanted and needed, something they never got at home anymore. Bo had the charisma and hunger for sex that made any man feel like they were the star in their own blue movie.

He never tired of a man falling in obeisance to his monstrous dick. If a man wasn't objectively handsome, Bo could find a small something about him and make it into a source of passion and desire. The man would feel wanted. But Bo had yet to discover the value of his skills; his career was only just about to begin.

Carl sent Bo to an address on Las Vegas Boulevard. It was a modern, sleek office complex. On the second floor was the door marked "Red Tail Furnishings." It wasn't a furniture store. Bo knocked. The door opened immediately. Standing in the doorway was a balding businessman with a cigarette, a five o'clock shadow, and a six o'clock whiff of whiskey on his breath.

"Bo? You the one Carl was going on about? Come in, come in! It's a hundred degrees out. I'm losing the A/C!"

Bo took in the office. There were few signs that anything shady happened there. The desk had a blotter, an ashtray, an inkwell, and some nice stationery arranged in a stack. But a second glance gave a glimpse into the real nature of the business. The blotter was covered in sexual doodles. The ashtray was in the shape of a cock and balls. A cup of condoms sat in the inkwell. And the paperweight keeping the stationery from blowing away was a bronze pair of boobs.

The balding man introduced himself as Franco and led Bo into a back room where a three-way mirror stood next to several racks of clothing. In the corner, a twin bed with a handmade quilt stood in stark contrast to the office setting. It looked like someone's grandmother slept there—maybe Franco's grandmother.

Franco said, "Look, Bo, the clothes gotta be nicer than these. Hang on." He took out a cloth measuring tape and began taking Bo's measurements, noting them with a pencil.

"Okay, I got a few things you can try on, but they ain't gonna fit you right. I'll call these measurements down to the tailor so he can pick you out some nice suits. It's Luigi's Tailors on Fremont, near the Gulch. Then you go to Bill Cody's for the Western Wear. None of these loose baggy dungarees. We want you in some tight Wranglers, ya dig?"

Bo thought that maybe there would have been a job interview. Again, he was half right. It wasn't so much an interview as a peep show.

"Okay, kid, Carl tells a lot of tall tales, so I ain't betting you got what he says you did. Lemme see."

Bo felt a bit awkward, wondering if he'd understood Franco correctly. "Take these off?"

Franco waved his hand in frustration. "Whadda ya think?" His Brooklyn mobster accent was the sexiest thing about him. Bo fixated on it, like he was wont to do.

"I'll just..." He undid his jeans and let them fall to the floor.

Franco's cigarette fell to the floor. "Jesus Christ Almighty! Carl wasn't joking. Oh Jeez. You're a goddamn circus act."

Bo didn't mind the insult. He was focused on Franco's face. It was awash with fear and envy. Not much desire, as far as he could tell, more a covetousness. Franco mopped his brow. He stooped to pick up his cigarette and shoved it back in his mouth.

"You ain't coming near me with that thing, but I gotta put you through the audition all the same. Now, make me believe you want me. Like real bad, see?"

Bo let Franco's accent take him somewhere far away on the East Coast. His eyes wandered across Franco's frumpy body until they fixed on his crotch. There was something noticeable there. A hint of something big. And Franco's waist was slim. His upper body was broad. He might be a bit muscular. As Bo fantasized about this man, his cock grew heavy.

Franco said, "So what, you into me or something?"

Bo nodded. "I could take you for a spin."

Franco laughed. "You got it, kid. You got the sex evil in you. I believed you for a second."

Bo blushed. He'd convinced himself he wanted Franco. "I wasn't bullshitting."

Franco glared at Bo, then snapped his fingers and laughed. "No man, you got it down good. I was half ready to jump in the sack with you just to see what you thought you were gonna do with me. I don't take it in the ass."

Bo said, "I do."

The words hung in the air like a smoldering cigarette. Franco chuckled, then stopped. He looked angry.

"I ain't no finocchio, kid. I don't swing that way. So if you're serious, just stop right there. You got the job. Don't piss me off."

Bo couldn't help himself. He'd found the things about Franco that excited him, and he wanted him. It was that simple. He couldn't exactly turn it off. His cock was hard now, hanging at a 45-degree angle in front of his body.

Bo saw Franco steal a tiny glance once, twice, a third time. He knew what to do next. It was baked into his being.

"You can touch it, you know, just to get a feel for it."

Franco looked ready to bite Bo's head off, but then he stopped. "You don't mind?"

Bo had him. The fish bit the hook. "Not at all."

Franco wiped sweat from his brow and stubbed out the cigarette. With one hand, he picked up the end of Bo's cock and squeezed it.

"Wow. It's a big son of a bitch. But you got that little head. Heck. My head's bigger'n that."

Bo smiled. "No. It can't be!"

Franco puffed out his chest. "It is."

"Prove it."

Franco loosened his belt and let his suit pants fall to the ground, revealing a short, very fat Italian cock. The head wasn't bigger, but it wasn't much smaller. "I ain't hard yet."

Bo heard the word 'yet' and knew he was in control. "Get it hard for me, Franco. Let's compare."

Franco licked his lips, admiring the show between Bo's legs. It was a turn-on, even for the least queer of men like Franco. Something about the power of Bo's cock transcended sexual preference. Its size was contagious, intoxicating, emboldening. Franco gave a few tugs, and his cock grew longer. The head swelled up and indeed grew a little bigger than the head of Bo's big torpedo.

Franco pounded his chest like an ape. "Ha! I told ya I got you beat."

Bo said, "It's pretty fucking thick. You ain't fucking me with that thing!"

Franco said, "Damn right I ain't. I told you I don't do that."

Bo turned around, pulling his butt cheeks apart. "You sure you don't want to test the goods before you put them on the market?"

He couldn't see Franco's face, but he could imagine it. Envy and fear were vanishing, replaced with the basic lust that makes a man want to stick his dick in a hole. Any hole. It was a crucial moment.

Bo knelt on the twin bed, ass in the air, cock draped across the mattress. "Come on, Franco, you know you need something. I didn't see a wedding ring on that finger."

"Fuck it." He felt Franco's rough hands take him by the waist. Franco spat on his cock, wiping the excess on Bo's hole. "You ready?"

Bo nodded. Wham! Franco had no technique. He rammed his fat cock in Bo's hole like he was slugging a fastball. Bo felt pain, but the satisfaction of seducing that man far exceeded any discomfort. Franco was fast. He pounded Bo a dozen times, then stopped. Holding his hips against Bo's backside, he grunted and dumped his load. He pulled out quickly, with a loud slurp.

Bo turned around. Franco's cock was still hard, throbbing in the air, covered with come. Bo knelt and cleaned it off with his tongue. Franco swatted him playfully.

"Hey, enough! I ain't doing that wit' you again, not ever." He pulled away, suddenly shy, as his shrinking cock when back into his suit pants. Bo stood, fully naked, in front of Franco.

Franco winked. "Kid, you got exactly what it takes. Welcome to the Red Tail family."

# NOAH

Bo started work three nights later. He picked up three suits from Luigi's and called Red Tail Furnishings from his hotel lobby.

"Red Tail, this is Franco."

"It's Bo."

There was a moment's hesitation. Bo chuckled to himself. Franco's distress over their dalliance was eating at him. "Yeah, Bo, good news, we got an all-nighter for you. At the Thunderbird. Room 45. You got cab fare?"

Bo said, "Sure. Do I wear a suit?"

Franco said, "Yeah. This guy's a high roller. He's gonna be busy gambling, but he'll want you ready when he gets back. Just kick back and listen to the radio until then. The key's at the front desk under the name Cottonwood. They're expecting you."

Bo scribbled down the information and hailed a taxi. The suit fit perfectly. He'd never worn tailored clothes before. This was a tight fit. The tailor was startled, but he knew just what to do with his cock. Bo picked a side. The tailor made the left leg a tad wider than the right. It didn't hide it, nor did it show it off. His left leg sported a massive bulge, but you had to look closely to really be sure. It felt good to be in properly fitting clothes that accommodated all his dimensions.

The Thunderbird was one of the first casinos on the

strip. It sported a colorful if not a bit childish sculpture meant to look like an Indian Thunderbird. Bo gave the name Cottonwood at the desk, and the clerk handed him a key and winked. He pointed him down the hall, past a noisy casino floor drowning in the din of a few hundred slot machines, clattering roulette wheels, and various shouts of joy or frustration.

The room was empty. A pair of suits hung in the closet. The radio was tuned to a station playing swing band music. It was pleasant and quiet, off the strip at the back. In the central courtyard, out of the sliding glass door, was an inviting pool. Bo made a mental note to bring a swimsuit next time.

Bo kicked off his loafers and lay outstretched on the bed. He dozed off. The door woke him. The man who came in was not particularly handsome. He was tall with a middle-aged spread, but he wore a suit that minimized his unfortunate shape and size. He had a hairy nose adorned with a handlebar mustache, and deep-set eyes that twinkled when he saw Bo.

"Hey, name's Noah Steinberg. And you are?"

"Bo." They didn't shake hands. Bo studied his date for the night. He looked for things to turn him on. He liked his manicured hands, his strong chin and jaw, and the slick haircut. And there was something fatherly about him. A kindness in his demeanor. That was enough to work with.

Noah said, "I know, not much to look at. But I like to fuck, so you don't have to look if it's too much for you."

Bo stood and took Noah's hand, caressing it, kissing it. "Hey, hey," Bo said, "I like a strong jaw." He patted Noah's chubby cheek. He took in the man's energy and let it go to his cock.

Noah took off his jacket and shirt, revealing a furry belly. Better. Bo was semi-hard now. It was more than enough.

Noah put a hand on the crotch of Bo's suit pants,

frowning when he encountered only a big pair of balls there. He looked down, eyes widening, following the path of the enormous cock down Bo's thigh.

"Oh, Jesus. You're big."

Bo loved a compliment. He stripped to the waist.

Noah clamped a mouth over Bo's nipple and gently bit it. "Good thing I don't take it up the ass."

Bo chuckled. "I do." He wanted to be whatever Noah needed him to be. It made him feel wanted, cared for, appreciated. He took hold of Noah's beautiful right hand and placed it on his bottom.

Noah rubbed Bo's muscled butt. "Oh man, that's fuckable, kid. Bend over."

Noah came around and studied Bo's bulbous ass, stroking himself. "God, I wanna fuck that."

Bo straightened, undoing the suit pants, kicking them off. His cock swung like a pendulum between his legs, slapping one knee, then the other.

"Geez, kid. That's the biggest fucking cock I ever seen."

"Wait 'til it gets hard."

Noah pushed Bo face forward into the bed and tongued his asshole. His mustache tickled. Bo wriggled, laughing to himself that he was getting paid to feel this good. Male attention was a drug. He was getting high. His cock, pressed against the bed and pointing towards the floor, was nearly hard.

When Noah shucked his suit pants, he sported a pink cock, not big, not small. Bo liked them any size, as long as they fit. Noah would be an easy lay.

Noah entered him easily with a grunt of satisfaction. Silence fell on the room, leaving only the distant sound of slot machines and the quiet, slippery noises as Noah's cock slid in and out. Bo broke the silence with a quiet groan of contentment.

"You like that?"

Bo nodded. "You're good at this."

Noah was slow, deliberate, and spent a lot of time

near Bo's prostate. Bo dribbled juice onto the carpeting from his now rock-solid cock. He reveled in the joy of penetration, connecting with Noah. It was palpable, the energy between them.

Noah remarked, "Wow, kid, you got something. I never felt that from nobody, not even my ex-wife."

Bo stayed motionless, letting Noah's skillful moves do their magic. The man was truly gifted. He knew just what pace to go to drive a man wild. It was just slow enough that Bo wanted it faster, and, paradoxically, it was just fast enough to make Bo twitch with pleasure. Bo wasn't sure if it was skill, or just luck that made Noah so good at fucking. Maybe that pace was exactly what Noah needed to get off, or maybe he was catering to his partner. Bo got the answer after fifteen minutes had elapsed. By then, he was writhing with delight.

"Kid, I gotta speed up so's I can get off, is that okay?

Bo said, "Fuck me, Daddy."

Noah held Bo's waist and pounded hard for a good five minutes. It made Bo crazy, it felt so damn good.

Noah said, "I'm gonna come soon."

"Do it."

A few loud, hard hip slapping cracks punctuated the final moments of Noah's work. Then he stopped, all the way inside. Bo felt the familiar warmth fill his ass. He reached down and stroked his own cock at an awkward angle.

Noah pulled out and rolled Bo onto his back. "Give me a show."

Bo stroked hard with both hands wrapped around his cock. Noah leaned in and gave a third helping hand, ever considerate of his partner. In two minutes, Bo was there.

"I'm gonna shoot."

Noah stepped back to watch. Bo's balls churned as his shaft throbbed and spouted a long, ropy jet of cum skyward. It came in waves.

Noah said, "Holy shit. I expected a dribble. You're really turned on, ain't ya?"

Bo nodded as more cum came, eventually slowing to a trickle. With both hands, Bo nursed the tip of his cock, letting the last droplets bead at the tip and run down the sides.

⚜

AFTER A SHOWER, NOAH SAID, "I GOT A GOOD feeling about you. Since I got you all night, let's hit the poker tables."

Bo said, "I don't know how to play poker."

"What? You live in Vegas and you can't play cards? That's a damn shame. Let me show you how, and then we'll go."

After a brief lesson, Bo got the gist. He was young, and it didn't take long to figure out the difference between a flush and a straight or a pair of eights and a pair of Kings. It was much easier than he'd imagined.

Bo said, "Remember, you don't make a move, lift an eyebrow, or nothing. They don't call it a poker face for kicks. It's a real thing. You got a tell, and you'll lose."

Bo said, "What if I mix it up: make 'em think I got a tell, but I switch it."

Noah said, "I think you're gonna be a natural. Of course that's what you do. Lose a couple hands, maybe win one, let them think you got a tell, then switch it all around. Keep them guessing. Scratch your nose, clear your throat, whatever. But I was gonna wait for that lesson. For now, just sit beside me and be my good luck charm. Watch how it's done."

Bo studied Noah's face while he cleaned up at a five-dollar table full of less experienced players. He watched for his fake tells, followed which cards he played, how many he asked for, how much he bet, and which hand won over another. After two hours, Noah cashed out a few thousand dollars richer.

"You think you got it down, kid?"

Bo said, "Yeah, I think so."

Noah said, "Alright, I'm gonna stake you fifty. If you lose it, it comes out of your tip. If you win, you pay me back and keep the rest. What do you say?"

Bo hadn't realized there would be any tipping. He was interested to see if he could win. It was late, close to midnight, but there were no windows and no clocks, so he didn't really care. He was dying to try it.

"Let's go over here to the rubes' tables." Noah led him to another area where the stakes were much lower. A fifty-cent minimum bet, and you could ante in twenty-five-cent increments.

Noah said, "I'm going back to the room, I'm bushed. I think you might be a natural, so don't disappoint me. You got the key. Don't wake me up."

Bo handed over the crisp fifty-dollar bill for a stack of poker chips.

With just the leanest lesson and two hours of observation, Bo had picked up the system. His sexual life had taught him to signal intentions, withhold emotions, and many other body tricks that translated well to poker. He intentionally lost a half dozen hands to learn the other players' tells. He was down almost thirty dollars. But it was intentional.

The seventh hand, he guessed what every other player was holding, and knew he had a fifty percent chance of holding a winning hand. He knew that one player was holding three high cards, hoping for a full house. Bo had a flush, and they were at ten dollars. When he won the hand, he was ahead. He kept following a random pattern of wins and loses, all intentional, and cleaned up. He had nearly $350.00 when he cashed out. That was more than he might make tonight. The Red Tail wasn't very forthcoming with their payment schedule.

Bo looked at the clock. It was nearly dawn. He

dragged himself to the bedroom and slipped in beside Noah, drifting off into a dreamless sleep.

Bo awoke slowly, wracked with pleasure. Noah was inside him, working his magic. It was ten in the morning; Noah was the perfect wake-up call. They both came together this time.

After a quick shower, Bo dressed, ready to head back to the Red Tail to drop off the money.

Noah lit a cigarette. "So, kid, how much did you make?"

Bo shrugged. "I have $350.00, give or take a few dollars."

Noah dropped the cigarette. "You're up three hundred? You're shitting me!"

Bo smiled. "I learned from a master."

Noah said, "Nah. Beginner's luck. We gotta try again."

Bo said, "I'm due back at the, uh, agency by noon."

"I'll drive you. Don't worry, I'll pay you for your time. I want to watch you."

Noah paid the Red Tail in advance for the entire weekend, a staggering sum of nearly two thousand dollars. While Noah waited, Franco took Bo to the back office to pay him. He gave him $800.00 for the previous night and the coming weekend. He clapped him on the back. "What'd you do, Bo? You rock his world?"

Bo shrugged. "He did most of the work. It's not about the sex; it's poker."

Franco frowned. "You gambling when you're working?"

"He asked me to."

Franco shrugged. "We frown on that, but it ain't illegal, exactly. So you won him over with your gambling skills?"

Bo shrugged. "You fucked me, what do you think?"

Franco glared at Bo, then laughed. "You're great in the sack. I think it's probably a little bit of both."

$ 6 %

# POOLSIDE

When they got to the Thunderbird, Bo slapped his knee. "Shoot! I forgot my swimsuit."

Noah said, "They got a store in the lobby. I'll get you one. I'd like to see that."

Bo said, "The new styles don't fit right."

Noah said, "Let's check it out. I'm sure they got something that'll work."

Luckily, there was a plaid Bermuda-length swimsuit by Catalina that would cover Bo as long as he didn't get hard. It came with a matching jacket.

"That's gonna look great. I wanna show you off by the pool."

Bo agreed. Noah spent a long time applying tanning oil to Bo's muscular body. He wore baggy trunks, but his hardon still showed.

Bo said, "You wanna fuck?"

Noah smiled. "You have to ask?"

An hour later, lounging by the pool, Bo got a lot of stares. The plaid didn't exactly hide what was in his shorts. It was stretched and distorted, and if he moved wrong, the head peeked out. But he found a comfort-able position and soaked in the rays. Noah lay beside him in a robe, covering his round, furry middle in a modest way that betrayed his wish to be built differently, more like Bo. But he had Bo in a chair next to him, which explained his satisfied smile. Ladies passed by, removing their sunglasses to stare unabashedly. Men, too. Bo was the personification of manhood with his bulging swimsuit and oiled-up muscles.

Bo turned to Noah and said, "You sure you don't mind this? I mean, I ain't exactly working, am I?"

Noah said, "Bo, you're making me happy. Just lie there like a show pony. I'm taking credit. A lot of these guys wish they were me right now."

Bo realized it was the first time Noah had called him by his name and not just 'kid'. It felt nice. He was more than just a prize-winning horse in Noah's stable. He was a person, too.

After some room service sandwiches, the two men got suited up and went down the hall to the casino.

"This time, Bo, you're gonna get two hundred from me, and you're sitting at the dollar tables. Be careful, there's a lot of card sharps there. That's the sweet spot for most professional players. I'll help you pick a table, but it's gonna change up and you might get tricked."

Bo sat at a table and immediately figured out who the sharps were. They were stony-faced, immovable, and unpredictable. Bo drove them crazy at first, but they were like him: able to discern when there was a bluff or a misdirected tell. Bo was down to thirty dollars when he figured out how to best the sharps. He didn't exactly flirt. Most couldn't help looking at his handsome face when they were studying his tells. He'd wink and throw them off their game, or he'd let his eyes get smoky and wet. It was a game of seduction, and it worked. By watching their reactions of disgust, desire, or lust, he picked out little facial tics that they couldn't control. And he parlayed his last thirty dollars (plus a twenty from his own stash) into a cool thousand. Even the sharps started throwing their hands down with a curse. Bo had beaten them at their own game.

Bo and Noah celebrated their wins with a steak

dinner at the Nugget. Bo enjoyed being in the company of a high roller. Noah shelled out a hundred to let Bo play a few games of pure chance, like craps and roulette. It wasn't as satisfying because Bo had no control over the outcome. It was just win or lose. No finessing could bring the ball to the right number or the right color. Betting against himself with a red number and a black square just made the whole thing worse. The dice weren't any better. He never got to a hundred after his first bet, so he stopped when he was down fifty dollars and gave it back to Noah.

"I'm sorry, I lost half."

Noah brightened. "You didn't lose, really. You learned two valuable lessons."

Bo gestured for him to go on.

"Yeah, so the first lesson, you don't gamble with chance, because you'll always come out behind. Poker is only half chance, maybe even less if you're good."

Bo said, "That's one. Okay."

Noah said, "You also quit when you were behind, which shows you know when to cut your losses. That's gold. It's priceless, and you did it instinctively."

Bo blushed. He liked how Noah handed out compliments.

Noah said, "May I ask you a personal question?"

Bo nodded.

"How much do they give you for a full night with me?"

Bo said, "Well, I got $800.00 for last night and the rest of this weekend."

Noah followed on. "And how much did you make tonight at one table?"

Bo did the math. "A thousand, less the hundred you spotted me."

"Right, so was it hard work?"

Bo shook his head. "It was almost as easy as getting fucked in the ass."

Noah turned red, choking with laughter. Bo joined him.

Noah said, "I ain't never been fucked, so I don't know what that means."

Bo said, "It's pretty fuckin' easy if you like it."

Noah leaned in. "Let's get a room right here, I need to feel that ass wrapped around my dick."

The Nugget doesn't rent by the hour, but the $30.00 was nothing to Noah. They got a room that overlooked the noise and bustle of Fremont Street. Noah cut the lights and let the neon paint the room with colorful patterns and flashes.

The bed at the Nugget was nicer than the one at the Thunderbird. When Bo lay face down, he could feel the difference in the coils and the ticking, like he was spread-eagled on a cloud. When Noah entered him, his eyes fluttered. Growing up in a shack in Arkansas, he'd never known luxury. He shed a bitter tear on the bed-spread, mourning a childhood of sorrow and misery.

"That feel good?" Noah asked, rhythmically pumping in that perfectly slow way that gave Bo chills.

Bo sniffed back another tear. "Yeah, Daddy, it's good." He hadn't meant to call him Daddy; it just came out. Noah was like the father he'd yearned for, not the drunk he'd grown up with.

Noah slapped Bo's ass. "You like it when Daddy fucks you, boy?"

Bo's cock leaped to attention. It had been harden-ing, but that slap and response was like Spanish Fly.

"Fuck me, Daddy. Make me come!"

Noah said, "Hold on a sec." He pulled out. He mo-tioned for Bo to lie on his back. Bo put his knees next to his ears. His towering cock partially blocked his view of his new daddy, Noah hooked his thumbs behind Bo's knees, pressing downward, until he could see past the huge cock.

"You jack off for your Daddy while he fucks you, Bo. I want to see your face when we come together."

Bo relaxed his legs, letting them drop further, until he could get both hands easily around his cock. He matched Noah's pace, up...down...up...down. It was almost too much. Bo had to stop and wait for a near orgasm to subside. A long, sticky trickle of juice oozed from his head. To his surprise, Noah lapped it up. Just feeling his tongue on his cock for that moment nearly did him in.

"You taste good, son."

Son. Bo held back more tears. *Was this tall, fat man with the unfortunate face the Daddy he deserved?* He didn't know, but his heart struggled to stem the tide of emotions.

"What's wrong, Bo? Did Daddy do the wrong thing?"

Bo shook his head vigorously. "No, it was so right."

Noah grinned. "That's gonna make me come."

He sped up his pace. Bo matched him. Together, they thundered toward a mutual orgasm. Bo loved that feeling from sex where both people were taking all they wanted from the other and getting even more back. Their breaths grew shallow.

"Ungh! I'm there! Ohh shit that feels good." Noah held himself tightly against Bo's butt, releasing inside him. At the same instant, Bo shot a skyward fountain of cum, showering both men.

Noah collapsed, breathing hard, his firm chin wedged between Bo's pectoral muscles. He smiled and, for the first time, kissed Bo. The kiss started small and smoldered until it was a raging fire of passionate love-making. They fell asleep in each other's arms.

❧  7  ❧

# WHAT IT TAKES

They returned to the Thunderbird, where they continued the lovemaking, sunbathing, and high rolling for the rest of the weekend. Bo could feel his heart break watching Noah pull out his suitcase.

"Where are you going?"

Noah said, "Next stop, Atlantic City. Then Monte Carlo. Then Mississippi. I have to move around to avoid running into the same sharps. Oh, we all move around. I'm hoping to put you on the circuit."

Bo's ears perked up. "Me? What do you mean?"

"You're a fresh face. You got natural talent. I'll front you the money and we split it. I get 75% and you get 25%. How does that sound?"

Bo hesitated. "What if I don't have what it takes?"

Noah patted him on the shoulder. "Oh, I know you do."

Bo said, "I'm not packed."

Noah laughed. "We gotta be careful about it. I don't want the Red Tail goons coming after me. You're their property right now. You probably signed a contract that violates the Thirteenth Amendment, but they're not exactly lawyers and judges."

Bo said, "What if I just pick up and leave?"

Noah said, "It'll cause you and me a lot of problems.

You need to get out of that contract first. I'll give you my P.O. Box in New York City. Write me when you're out from under them."

Bo felt trapped. He'd barely glanced at the contract. "How do I do that?"

Noah said, "Maybe work for them for a few months more, and then make up a family emergency. Sick relative...you're gonna be gone for a long time. Something like that."

Bo fought back tears as he watched the nicest man in Vegas pack his bags. He hugged him. Noah patted him on the shoulder. "Don't worry, kid. We'll be together someday soon. And watch it with the crying. It'll fuck with your poker face. And stay away from the tables. I don't want the sharps to clock you."

# 8

## WILL IT FIT?

Bo hadn't worked a regular shift yet. He'd lucked out on his first date, a long weekend, and now he had to work for real. Monday night, he called in, and there was a job waiting at Binion's Horseshoe, two blocks from his bachelor's quarters. As he got ready, a knock on his door startled him.

"It's Grayson. You got a minute?"

Bo opened his door, shirtless, in a hurry, and happy to see Grayson's winning smile.

"Yeah, what's up?"

"Can I borrow ten dollars? I'm short on rent."

Bo was flush. He took out a ten and handed it to him. "Keep it. I wouldn't want you to get to where you couldn't pay rent because you had to pay me back. It's a gift."

"Wow. Thanks, man. I really appreciate it." Grayson stood staring at Bo. He didn't say anything, just stared.

"Is there something else?"

"Nothing. I mean, okay. I can't stop thinking about that cock of yours. Ain't run into you since that first night."

Bo nodded. He remembered how good it felt when Grayson lifted his hip and let Bo find his way to that previously unknown inner paradise. He felt blood rush to his cock.

Grayson said, "I heard you found some work. I've done that, but not for an agency or nothin'. You like it?"

Bo said, "I got a job right now. Sorry, Grayson, I want to fuck you bad, but I need to save myself, you know?"

Grayson twisted the tip of his boot in a knothole in the rug, not meeting Bo's eyes. "I just ain't ever been with someone that made me feel that way."

Bo put a hand on his shoulder. "We got all the time in the world. I can't give you my heart, but I'll give you my dick. Yeah?"

Grayson brightened up. "It's a deal!"

At the Horseshoe, Bo gave his passcode to the clerk, who solemnly passed him a key.

"Third floor."

Room 312 was at the back of the hotel, away from the noise and bustle of Fremont Street. Bo opened the door. The client was sprawled out on the bed, jerking his cock. He was in his thirties, furry hair, muscular body, and a big dick. He looked like he could work for Red Tail. He wasn't what Bo expected. Bo had no trouble finding sexy details to get him hard. Least of all the big dick, which looked like fun, but maybe hard work.

"What's that in your pants? Is that your dick?"

The man sat up, fascinated.

"Yeah man, my dick." Bo unfastened his pants and let them drop, revealing his half-hard cock. The man crawled backward on the bed in startled amazement.

"Oh my god, that's a beautiful work of art. Praise Jesus."

Bo smiled, growing a little longer and stiffer at the compliment.

"I'm Bo. And you're..."

"Reggie. Oh man, I was really hoping to take it up the ass, but that's just not gonna fit."

Bo said, "Well, you'll just have to fuck me, then."

Reggie nodded. I will, but I really want to see you

fuck SOMEONE with that. I mean, it's just got to go somewhere. I'll call the agency and order up another. He reached for the hotel phone.

Bo put a hand out. "Stop. You might not find anyone who can take it, but I got someone in mind. How much you paying?"

"I gave them a hundred. I'll add fifty if you bring a friend."

Bo knew he was probably violating Red Tail's policy, but he was being practical. "Wait here. I'll be back in ten. Don't tell the agency I'm doing this."

As Bo waited for the elevator, he thought about the price the man quoted. A hundred? Did that mean Bo was making less than 50 bucks himself? What happened to that big paycheck with Noah? He had half a mind to call up the agency, but he was on the clock.

Grayson jumped at Bo's offer. He was still in his cowboy outfit from the Pioneer. They hoofed it two blocks and made it back to 312 in just under ten minutes.

Reggie opened the door when he heard them approaching. He was still stark naked, his long, fat cock jutting from between his legs. Bo had some work to do this time. He didn't care. He still loved a big dick, even if he'd fallen for a guy with nothing but a regular dick and unbelievably good technique.

Bo realized the man had nothing to make it go in easy, and breathed a sigh of relief when Grayson produced a small tub of Albolene.

Reggie lay on his back, his cock slick with spit and grease. Bo squatted facing him, smiling as he sat on it. Reggie couldn't help but touch the monstrous meat towering in his face. He brought it forward and peppered it with kisses. Bo felt it reach the back of his ass with a little more to go. He leaned to the left and felt it pass partway through the curtain before he reached Reggie's lap.

Reggie pressed upwards. It was a bit awkward, and

grew more so when Grayson stood on tiptoe and put the head of Bo's dick in his ass.

Reggie said, "Will it really fit?"

Grayson nodded and began the long, slow ride down Bo's gargantuan pole. He twisted and let Bo inside him all the way. He bent his knees and straightened them, riding up and down the length of Bo's cock.

Reggie said, "Amazing. Praise Jesus."

Bo wondered if the guy was a holy roller on a sinful excursion. Grayson got hard. Reggie greedily put the pretty pink dick in his mouth, his head bobbing up and down in sync with Grayson's ride up and down Bo's cock.

The three way fuck with Bo in the middle was clunky and cumbersome. Bo put on his best smile and made sure Reggie felt like a king. That was his job. Grayson had no need to feign a smile. He was in a state of rapturous bliss, riding the cock he'd craved for nearly a week.

Reggie put his hands under Grayson's cheeks, assisting by lifting and lowering him. He let Grayson's dick fall from his mouth.

Reggie said, "I can taste it, you're almost there, aren't you?"

Grayson nodded.

"Shoot it on my face."

Grayson yanked on his dick a few times, then ejaculated all over the client. Not just his face, but his furry chest, his lap, and his hair.

Reggie said, "What a naughty boy you are. Pastor's gonna give you a whippin' after this."

They switched positions. Now Reggie was behind Bo, fucking him. Grayson lay on his back, looking into Bo's eyes. Bo impaled him, marveling at how his cock formed a lump in the cowboy's stomach. Grayson was hard again, flogging his cock. Bo felt himself getting too turned on.

Reggie said, "I'm close. Are you?"

Bo and Grayson said, "Yes" at the same time.

"Here it comes." Reggie pulled out and shot his sperm on Bo's back.

Grayson said, "I'm ready. Come inside me."

But Reggie said, "No, no. You pull out and shoot on him."

Grayson couldn't hide his frown, but Bo kept a smile on his face. "Yes, sir."

He pulled out, jerking his cock with one hand as best he could. He splattered Grayson's face. Grayson stopped jacking off and his cock grew soft. He didn't have a second load after all. Or maybe he did have it, and he'd needed Bo inside him to come.

The man's two hours were up. He gave Bo $150.00 and no tip. He picked up the Bible and began reading aloud to himself from Leviticus. Bo and Grayson scampered out before the scene got any stranger. Bo gave Grayson $50.00, hoping it would be enough. It was.

Grayson said, "Can I walk you home?"

"I gotta bring this to the agency." He hailed a cab. It turned out he only got $40.00. It was something, but not like playing the tables or tricking with a high roller.

# 9

# LETTERS

Weekdays were slow. Weekends were busy. Bo rarely had dates on Monday, Tuesday, or Wednesday. He usually had two on Thursday, and three a night on Friday and Saturday. Sundays were more of a daytime gig with just one or maybe two if he was lucky. It continued for weeks. He never stopped enjoying sex, but he realized he missed feeling loved. Over the next two months, he slept with dozens of men. Maybe over a hundred. He didn't spend much of what he earned, and he wondered when he could leave it behind and be with Noah. He started to doubt that Noah was serious. It just crept into his head and stayed there.

Two letters arrived on the same day. One letter came from New York. Noah wrote:

Dear Bo,

It feels empty here without you. Have you told the agency yet? They can't keep you if it's a family thing. I need you near me. Call me. I'm here for two weeks.

Love,
N

BO WAS SO EXCITED! THEN HIS STOMACH TURNED when he saw the letter from Arkansas. It was his Aunt Bev.

Bo,

Sorry to say your father passed from liver failure. We had the funeral already. Figured you didn't want to go, seeing how you aren't a family member any more. We're all sorry you threw your life away. But it's your life.

Aunt Bev

BO DIDN'T SHED A TEAR. HE PUT ON HIS BEST SAD face and hopped in a taxi to Red Tail. Franco was behind the desk, playing with the cock-shaped ashtray. He smiled when Bo walked in.

"Hey, if it isn't the cock of the walk! What brings you here on a Monday?"

Bo forced out an Oscar-worthy sob. "It's my Pa. He's in a real bad way. They say he ain't got long to live."

Franco came around the desk and gave a comforting hug.

"Can I go home to say goodbye? He's got no one to look after him. I might need to stay a while."

Franco said, "Of course. You go take care of you, and come back soon. We'll manage. You're a top-notch hustler, and don't you forget it. When you're back, we'll be waiting for you."

Bo wiped some crocodile tears from his eyes and thanked Franco profusely. He rushed out the door, never looking back.


WITH HIS THINGS ALL PACKED, BO WAITED AT THE train station. He'd arrived in Las Vegas in a stinky, crowded bus and was leaving on a fancy train. He'd sprung for a private room. If he was going to be stuck somewhere for three days, it might as well be nice. He dropped a letter in the mailbox addressed to a P.O. Box in New York City. He hoped it would arrive before he did.


THE END

# ABOUT THE AUTHORS

**J. W. Steed** is a pseudonym for the author of more than a dozen mainstream novels. He also writes memoir and humorous essays. He teaches creative writing in the metro NYC area and is active in the Science Fiction and Fantasy Writer's Association (SFWA). Steed made his paperback debut in the bestseller <u>Dirty Dorms and Fresh Men</u>. He has a cult following who can't wait to read more! You can read Mr. Steed's blog at: mrsteed64.blogspot.com

**Chuck Idgaf** is a relatively new queer author. Deep into middle age, Chuck decided to broaden his hobbies, writing very erotic short stories. Initially, he just shared them with friends. The collaboration with Jim Dandy is the first time his work will be widely available. Chuck has a fondness for bears and daddies, so those tend to be common themes. He also likes stories about coming out, first times, and exploring new experiences. If you can't figure it out from the dialogue in his stories, Chuck grew up in the Deep South. He now lives in the Coachella Valley, California, with his husband.

**Peter Schutes** is the nom de plume of a prolific and acclaimed novelist. As Peter Schutes, he is the author of Adult Erotic Fiction such as <u>The Slaves of Rome</u>, <u>Dark as a Dungeon</u>, <u>The Gospel of Priapus</u>, and <u>Panama Heat</u>. He writes in the style of vintage pulp authors from the 1960s and 1970s. He lives in Los Angeles. You can read many of his stories on his world wide web page at peterschutes.com

Dutch Treat

Enjambment

The Expectant Member

Filthy Jobs and Steamy Showers

Firehouse Lovers

The Fish

Five Erotic Tales

The Good Dad

The Gospel of Priapus

Hardhats and Nightsticks

Hercules and Lippos

Hobo Honey

Hoboes, Hustlers, and Outlaws

Hot Blue Collars

Hotshot

In Each Other's Arms

Joker's Wild

Kwiklube 5000

Like the Greeks Do

Little Shamus

Logger's Delight

Muscle Beach

Muscle Bottom

One Eternal Day

The Orchardman

Panama Heat

Satanic Seductions

Satan's Sissy Boy

The Slaves of Rome

Sleazy A

Small Cockpits and Big Hangars

The Spotter

Steroid Steve

Tales of Two Daddies

The Tearoom in the Trees

The Thigh Baby

Tuxes n' Tails

Under the Boardwalk

Wee Dobbin

World's Biggest

***** Coming Soon *****

More Tales of Two Daddies

Mowing and Blowing

www.ingramcontent.com/pod-product-compliance
Lightning Source LLC
Chambersburg PA
CBHW010600310726
48969CB00009B/2511